GARGOYLE DREAMS

A GOTHIC LOVE STORY

DUNCAN McGEARY

Edited Lara Milton
Cover by Andy Zeigert

First Edition - 2024

Chapter 1

Peter bounded down the spiral staircase, taking two and three steps at a time and leaping the last five. His feet slipped on the smooth marble, and he sprawled forward and slid across the floor. He scrambled to his feet and sprinted through the nave toward the big front doors.

He didn't hear them chasing him, but then, he hadn't heard them approaching at all until they were nearly upon him. They had glided across the floor, impossibly silent. But he'd sensed their murderous intent.

A few minutes before, he'd thought he was about to make love to his girlfriend. Oh, he knew it was likely she was going to break up with him, but that was no reason not to take advantage of a little last-minute guilt sex. Mary was predictable that way.

But instead, she'd confronted him about the phone messages from Jan. Peter had managed to turn the conversation back to money, like he always did. After all, money was the problem, not his dalliance with his secretary.

He'd driven by the cathedral a thousand times, since he lived on the same street, but he'd never actually walked by it, much less entered it. Mary had been silent as they'd walked toward the huge, dilapidated structure. As far as he knew, nobody actually attended services there anymore. It was some kind of administrative center. Or maybe it was used for storage.

Mary led him toward the back of the cathedral, but just before they reached the loading dock, she ducked behind some brown and dying hedges and opened a small door, recessed in a corner, that looked like it was hardly ever used.

"I found this by accident," she said. "It leads straight to the rooftop. You've really got to see this. But be quiet. I don't think we're supposed to be here."

They entered an unlit room with a narrow doorway to one side, with spider webs in the corners and thick dust on the walls. There were footprints down the middle of the floor—they looked like Mary's footprints, Peter realized, though he wasn't sure how he knew that. How often had she been coming here? He started to ask, but she put her finger to her lips and shushed him.

A narrow set of stairs led up to the main floor. Mary stopped him before she entered, poking her head out, and then waved him on. There were broader marble steps inside, spiraling up above the main floor, narrowing as they went higher, until toward the top, they were so narrow that they had to walk single file.

Mary led Peter out onto the rooftop. There was a catwalk along one side. Peter could see the huge ears and gnarled heads of gargoyles perched just below it, running the length of the nave. Then she turned to him abruptly and, as he'd feared, confronted him about Jan.

"Jan doesn't mean anything to me and you know it," he said. "She's an airhead."

"It means something that you cheated," she replied, and her tone of voice told him it was truly over. "The fact that you feel nothing for her only makes it worse."

He felt a strange sense of relief. "Look," he said. "If you want me to move out, just say so."

"We rented that apartment together," she said. "I can't afford it alone."

"Then you can't afford to quit your job either," he countered.

That was the underlying reason for the argument, the reason they had been drifting apart for the last few months. Mary hated her job and wanted to quit. But her job, even as a lowly office worker, paid nearly as well as his job. He was still an intern at his law firm, though the partners had promised him a position upon graduation. The big money would come later. Until then, they needed the money her job could bring in.

"What are you going to do?" Peter asked. "Get a minimum-wage job somewhere? That won't cut it, and I'll be damned if I will pay the full rent."

"Instead, you want to leave and stick me with the rent?" Mary asked incredulously.

"It's your name on the lease," he said smugly.

Mary slapped him hard. Peter hadn't seen it coming. She'd never been violent before; in fact, he would have bet everything that she didn't have it in her. Reflexively, he struck back, smashing a fist into her nose. It spurted blood.

Bad enough, but maybe he could've explained it away, since she'd struck him first. But he punched her again, and blood splashed onto the catwalk and over the side of the cathedral.

Then he backed away from the look in her eyes.

"I'll move out tonight," Peter muttered. He turned to leave. Mary was sobbing loudly behind him, but he kept going. He didn't remember descending the stairs and couldn't figure out how he'd gotten lost, but he found himself in an unfamiliar hallway. He looked back, but couldn't see the stairs. He retraced his steps and was confronted by a blank wall.

How the hell did that happen?

There were low voices chanting in a nearby room. The door was slightly ajar, and a flickering light emanated through the crack. Peter pushed the door open another couple of inches and poked his head in, intending to ask for directions.

The room was full of gargoyles, like those he'd seen above, but these were of all shapes and sizes. The candlelight seemed to make them move, their ghostly expressions looking malevolently alive. A half-dozen cloaked figures stood amid the gargoyles, chanting in a foreign language.

Latin, Peter thought, then changed his mind. *No, it's too guttural and harsh to be Latin.*

3

In his surprise, Peter pushed the door open a tiny bit more and a shrill screech filled the small space, and as one, the cowled figures turned his way. Peter was running before his mind could fully register what he'd seen.

What did *I see?* Now he could only remember the blackness within the robes, but at the time…he'd seen squirming tentacles whipping toward him, reaching for him.

As he got up from his fall at the base of the stairs, he saw the small door that he and Mary had come through, but something made him run toward the center of the cathedral and the daylight he could see from the open doors at the entrance. He sprinted down the worn red carpet between the pews and reached daylight, and suddenly his panic seemed foolish.

Once outside, he stopped and bent over, trying to get his breath. There were broad steps down to a crumbling sidewalk. Home—if only home for a few more hours—was just a few blocks away.

What did I really see? he asked himself again, but this time in the full light of day. It now seemed foolish to have been afraid. *It was probably just a bunch of priests, monks or something, praying,* he thought. *Just doing their thing.*

He straightened up and laughed. He was free. Mary had been a weight on his back for months now. She'd been useful in helping pay his way through law school, but she seemed to think that there was a promise there, that he'd marry her, take care of her.

Well, we're both adults. She has a good job. I don't need to feel guilty.

Peter practically skipped down the steps. There were large elm trees on either side of the entrance, and their roots were pushing up the concrete, leaving a small corridor near the cathedral's walls.

He heard a cracking sound and looked up to see a grotesque visage bearing down on him, as if a demon had come alive and was coming to take him away. He barely had time to cry out before it smashed into his forehead, cleaving his head in half before smashing into the stump of his neck. He topped backward into one of the elms, which held his body upright for a moment before it slid down. His blood spilled out onto the concrete, but seemed to find its way into the cracks, as if the gnarled roots were thirsty.

Dominic awoke.

How long had he slumbered?

Summer sun beat down upon his stone head, but he paid no attention to it, any more than he had the rains of spring or the freezing snows of winter. None of it mattered, not the weather nor the passing of time nor the constantly growing traffic on the streets below him. He slept year after year, barely aware he was alive.

Oh, his eyes were always open, but they didn't see, just as his overlarge ears could take in sound but not hear; just as his tongue, jutting from his mouth, broken at the tip, could sense the rain but not taste it. And then, in an instant, he was awake.

What had awoken him after so long?

He was vaguely aware of the human couple arguing above him, but it wasn't the first time, and nothing before had mattered. Something else had woken him, as if he had heard someone he once knew calling out to him. Loud, angry voices came from above, a man and a woman. The man was screaming at the woman, and she was protesting just as loudly, but there was something vulnerable in her voice, as if she knew or feared what was coming.

It was unusual for members of the public to be up there—forbidden by signs and locks—but somehow this man and woman had managed to sneak by the barriers, to carry on their argument alone in the middle of the city, above the congregants below and the nonbelievers rushing by outside.

Dominic heard the smack of the angry man's fist upon the woman's face, the smashing of her nose, and then...a single drop of blood flew over the side of the cathedral, dropping past the other, larger gargoyles with their huge drain spouts, past the arched stained-glass windows, past the nesting pigeons, to land on the head of a small, neglected gargoyle, half-hidden by the tall elms that had burst through the sidewalk below. It landed in the gargoyle's right eye.

Dominic was jolted fully awake, completely aware of his surroundings and of himself for the first time in two centuries. In an instant, Dominic knew everything there was to know about the woman. He knew that she was in danger and that she was alone

Her name was Mary Patronis, and he was meant to save her, and in the saving, he would himself be saved.

He saw the world through her eyes, through her tears. She moved to the side of the catwalk and stared down, intending to watch Peter walk away forever.

A few minutes later, Peter emerged from the cathedral and ran down the steps. Dominic heard a loud crack. From the corner of his eye, he saw the gargoyle, his long-mute companion who mirrored his own position on the other side of the cathedral doors, come loose. Then it was as if the carving jumped, plummeting to the earth. Below, the man was paralyzed by fear.

The gargoyle crashed down on him, seeming to break both statue and man into pieces.

Dominic's vision was fixed, but he could still see the turmoil below. Mary rushed out of the cathedral, crying out as she saw the body at the base of the elm tree. She stopped short of the body, staring down at the decapitated corpse in horror.

Help her! Dominic thought.

As if in response, a man hurried across the busy street and pulled her away as sirens approached in the distance.

Chapter 2

Dominic sensed Mary coming long before she came into view. The boulevard was long and straight, and he was frozen in such a position that he could see most of the distance to a statue of some long forgotten war hero, and what features he couldn't see easily, he had filled in by years of study, catching a broken stone shining in the low sun one day, the high branch of a tree in the last rays of an autumn twilight on another day, until he had memorized every square inch of what was possible to see.

Most visitors to the cathedral came from the side nowadays, parking their cars in the parking garage one block over. Dominic caught only glimpses of the parishioners as they darted into view below him and then into the building. People had sped up over the last few decades, flickering in and out of his line of sight like so many birds, and about as important to him. The pigeons shat on his head and the humans spewed poison into the air, and he could feel the acids from both eating into his stone body, but he couldn't do anything about either indignity.

He felt her coming from the moment she first had the impulse: waking up, taking a shower, deciding that she hadn't lit a candle in the church for a long time. Putting on sensible clothes and forgoing makeup, since she didn't expect to meet anyone she knew, either along the way or inside the cathedral itself. No one she knew went to church of any kind.

7

It was a residual compulsion on her part, a forlorn hope that maybe it did some good, that maybe a prayer and a thought and a lit candle and a little dust on her knees as she knelt would do some good, that Peter would escape the hell he no doubt deserved.

Was it a blessing or a curse that the gargoyle felt her emotions, sensed her thoughts and desires, suffered with her when she was hurt, exulted when she was triumphant? He himself wasn't sure. He'd been in a dim fog for many decades before she came into his existence, happily miserable or miserably happy to merely exist, forgetting his origins, forgetting that he had ever been human and able to move and think and feel.

Would he have been better off if she had never come along?

Dominic questioned it, but he always came to the same conclusion. It didn't matter. He now only existed because of her. Without Mary Patronis, he was just a rock on a wall, carved into a shape that had once been meant to frighten children and sinners, but which in the modern age was a curiosity, a whimsical reminder of a more primitive, fundamental past. His consciousness would have eventually flickered out completely, and he would have been glad of it. The world had no need of him, and he had no need of the world.

Now he was more vibrantly alive than at any time since he'd been cursed into this shape—vibrant in his senses, if not his movements. He sensed the workmen on the other side of the cathedral, striving as always to prop up the bulky walls with reinforcements, pinning the broken stones together to last yet another century, when new technology would patch the giant edifice together for yet another century. There was always the steady drumbeat of hammers and chisels, but where once it had lulled Dominic into a dreamless sleep, it now helped keep him awake, forever conscious of Mary Patronis and her infrequent religious whims.

He lived for these fitful days. Her blood was his blood, her thoughts were his thoughts, her body was his body. He walked with her, feeling the freedom of movement as an ecstatic felt the presence of God.

She was coming, and he longed to break free of his perch, to fly to her side, to rub his gnarled head against her. It would free him, he sensed. She would turn him back into a man with a simple touch.

But it was impossible, of course. Even if he could move, she would flee screaming from a nightmare come alive. Her fear would freeze him in place, just as his creator had intended. He was the manifestation of human fears and desires, locked into a shape that was a reminder of sin, but could not sin itself. The gargoyle was stuck between the living and the dead, a reminder to both.

The dead, at least, recognized him. They teased him sometimes with their freedom of movement, swirling about him, but he ignored them. Ghosts were less substantial than he, and they knew it in the remnants of their hearts and souls. And remnants were all the dead were left with if they chose to stay on the mortal plane, whereas the gargoyle was alive inside, bursting with hope and love.

All for Mary Patronis. All because of a drop of blood.

It had burst from the light of her, the love and the frustration she was feeling, so strong and pure of emotion that the gargoyle almost broke free.

Would he have flown in freedom or plummeted to the sidewalk to shatter? He'd moved a few centimeters, he was certain. He could see parts of the boulevard after that day that he had never seen before.

Impossible.

"You shall be stone," the priest had said. "You will never again feel movement. You will linger forever, frozen in purgatory. And be damned with you."

The man turned gargoyle, who had once been known as Dominic Carmelo, had secretly believed the punishment to be fair and just at the time. But even as his features changed, showing the anguish of that curse, he had fought against it. Not because he didn't deserve it, but because he wanted to die instead. The agonies of hell were more appropriate than the timelessness of purgatory.

The drop of blood from Mary Patronis had awoken his guilt, but something else had also happened: the chance of redemption had appeared. Dominic's long years of reflecting on his guilt and his sins had given him a small measure of wisdom, and inside, he knew that he would never again be the evil man he had once been. Given the chance, he would do good.

Mary Patronis had given him that gift.

9

And he loved her for it.

Chapter 3

Mary lit a candle, asking herself why she was doing it. Peter had been an asshole. She'd supported him all the way through law school, and when it came time to graduate, he'd started cheating on her. He had been set to begin earning a high income while she would have been left with pretty much nothing.

Why should she pray for his soul? Why should she even care?

I don't care, she thought. *Yet here I am.*

The cathedral was comforting. The gargoyles that decorated its walls didn't scare her. It was as if it was filled with ghosts of the past, who were watching her. She walked through those tall doors, and it was as if she was home. These ghosts were on her side. The first time she had walked by, she'd been drawn in. Later, she'd brought Peter, who was a lapsed Catholic. After that, whenever they had a fight, she would retreat here—until that last time, when he'd followed her up to the roof.

When he'd struck her, it had felt as if the ghosts of the cathedral had rallied around her in the spectral support, and she had heard herself telling him to leave: "I never want to see you again."

He'd grunted "Good," and left.

Mary had sat on the edge of the roof for a long time, crying, and it had felt as if the gargoyles around her had watched her in sympathy.

Why are they on my side? If they only knew what I do at work. Why don't they haunt me instead?

Because I'm a good person, she answered herself. *Because I do my best. Because...*

She had to believe that much, at least. She'd lost faith and hope along with everything else, but she had to try to still believe that being a good person was reward enough, if not in this life, then in the next.

You don't believe there is a next life.

Mary shook her head. She'd given up trying to understand herself, but her feelings toward her now-dead ex-boyfriend were probably some of the least confusing. She had loved him once and had thought there was still a chance he might pull his head out of his ass someday, until the freak accident with the gargoyle had ended his somedays for good.

And now you're lighting a candle to save his soul?

She laughed ruefully, and it echoed in the nearly empty vastness of the chamber. Lighting a candle for Peter was really just an excuse to visit the cathedral. An old woman sitting on a bench a few yards away frowned at her, and Mary gave her an embarrassed look.

"Where are you visiting from, Sister?" The question came from behind her, and she rose and faced the young priest smiling down at her.

She immediately realized why he'd made his mistake. She'd worn old clothes, sensible shoes, no makeup, and her hair was under a scarf. But she couldn't figure out a way to tell him the truth without embarrassing him. Could she pull it off?

"I'm...from here," she said.

"Funny, I thought I knew everyone in the city." He spoke with a slight Scottish brogue. He stared at her with a fixed smile, then a rosy glow began in his cheeks and spread over his round face. He was a little on the heavy side, and his hair was a little long, the way it looked when someone neglected his usual haircut. He had stylish sideburns and bright green eyes. "Oh, my gosh. Don't tell me...you're not a nun, are you?" It was more a statement than a question.

Something about his innocent embarrassment made her giggle. When was the last time she'd seen a man blush? "Far from it, Father. I'm not even Catholic."

Mary could feel him examining her, and she turned away. She always dressed down, though maybe not as much as today. She hid herself in as plain an appearance as possible, because when she dressed up and wore makeup, she looked like a model. She was a true blonde, with bright blue eyes, high cheekbones, and a nose just long enough to keep her face from looking perfect. Looking like a model caused more complications than it was worth.

"Well, the offer still stands," the priest said. "I'd be happy to give you a tour of the cathedral, places most people don't see. I'm Father Gregory, by the way."

"Mary Patronis."

He laughed. "A good Latin name, at least."

"Where are *you* from, Father Gregory?" she asked as he motioned her to follow him to one side of the church.

"I came here from Edinburgh when I was a student," he said, descending some wide marble stairs. "I never went back. And you, Mary? What do you do for a living?"

She felt a chill go through her. She came here because she wanted to forget what her job was. If she thought too much about that, it would spoil this place.

"I'm a secretary," was all she said.

He led her through the catacombs below the cathedral, which were strangely homespun. The rooms had modern fixtures and furniture, and the stone and brick was covered up as much as possible, as if the place's gothic origins had been smothered in a soft blanket.

The second-floor naves were ornate and aged, and the old, familiar feeling of peace came over Mary.

Father Gregory was watching her. "Are you sure you aren't Catholic?" he asked.

"Maybe in spirit," she said.

"Well, that is the point, isn't it?" he laughed. "Just let me know when you want to convert, and I'm your priest. It is refreshing to meet such an innocent. You wouldn't believe some of the things I hear."

"Innocent?" Mary laughed. "Believe me, Father, I'm no virgin."

"You know, I think there has always been a misunderstanding about that. I've known prostitutes with the proverbial heart of gold,

13

and I've known virgins with hearts as black as coal. I think what is required is not an intact hymen but a pure soul."

"Not sure I qualify there either," Mary said.

"Oh, but you do, Mary Patronis," Father Gregory said. "I can see into your heart, and it is kind and forgiving."

He led her to some narrow stairs that wound, spiraling, toward the ceiling. "I've got a real treat for you," he said. "Something few people have seen."

He led her out onto the roof. The city spread out below them, bustling and noisy. They were high enough and far enough away from the action that they were in an island of peace. Huge gargoyles dotted the edges of the roof, and other mythical creatures were carved into the stone of the roof itself. It was as if they were greeting her.

"I have a confession to make," Mary said. "I've been here before. I snuck up here when you were doing repairs."

"We never *stop* doing repairs," Father Gregory laughed. "Well, since you used the word 'confession,' I guess I'll have to absolve you."

She looked out over the city, and a feeling of peace again came over her. She must have been Catholic in some past life. Everything about this cathedral felt like home.

"It has a holy spirit, doesn't it?" Father Gregory said quietly.

"Yes," she said. "It's almost enough to make me a believer."

He didn't answer, simply stood companionably at her side for a time. Then he touched her lightly on her shoulder.

"I have to get back to work, Mary," he said. "But the next time you decide to light a candle, come look me up. I always have hot coffee in my office. I think you're a closet Catholic, and it won't take much to turn you to our side."

"If you keep being so nice, I may have to join the church just because I'll owe you."

"I can think of worse reasons," he said. "Besides, I think once you join, you'll find other reasons."

He let her go first, and as she descended the stairs, she saw a room to one side that she hadn't noticed before. A horrible face stared out at her, giving her a fright.

"What's that?" she asked.

Father Gregory almost bumped into her. He looked over, confused, and then smiled. "As I said, this place is always being repaired. That's where they put the construction materials."

Mary walked down the short passage to the room and went in. Along with blocks of granite and tiles and piles of wood, there were gargoyles lying about in every nook in cranny. They looked neglected, as if they'd been pushed to the side, and many of them were toppled over, looking forlorn.

"Why are the gargoyles here?" Mary asked.

Father Gregory grimaced. "They were taken down during repairs. The plan was to clean them up, perhaps even get some replacements, but there are a bunch of members of the parish who would rather they didn't go back at all."

"Oh, no!" she exclaimed. "You have to put them back. Your cathedral isn't a cathedral without them."

"Okay, now I *know* you're kidding me," Father Gregory said. "Only a true Catholic would say that."

"They really shouldn't be treated that way," Mary found herself saying. "It's very undignified."

"Well, they're gargoyles. They don't care."

"Are you so sure?" she asked. Father Gregory looked at her oddly, and she laughed as if she was making a joke.

Mary walked companionably by the priest's side toward the front entrance. As they passed through the main chamber, she saw the confessional booths to one side, and something made her blurt out, "Do you ever hear confessions from those not in the faith?"

Father Gregory stopped dead in his tracks, and Mary kept going a few paces before she realized she was alone. She turned back to see a concerned look on his face.

"I felt you were trying to escape something," he said. "The church can be very nurturing to those in need."

"I'm sorry," she said. "I was just curious. It was a stupid question."

"Not stupid at all," he said. "Come sit with me. I can't hear your confession, not officially, but I can listen to you as a friend, and I can promise you no one will ever hear anything about it from me."

So they sat in a pew, and Mary told him about the men she worked for, and how she suspected—no, how she *knew*—that they were crooked, and worse, that they were dangerous.

"What do I do?" she asked when she was done. "I need this job."

"No job is worth losing your soul—or if you aren't a believer, Mary, no job is worth losing your integrity," Father Gregory said solemnly.

"But if I quit, they'll just keep doing what they're doing," Mary argued. "I won't have accomplished anything."

"You could go to the authorities," he suggested.

She frowned. Despite her telling Father Gregory the basics of her dilemma, he really didn't understand the danger she was in. *It isn't his problem*, she thought. *This was a stupid thing to do.*

"You're probably right," she said brightly, standing up. He got up more slowly, as if waiting for her to tell him more. When she didn't say anything further, he started leading her to the front doors of the church.

She went down to the sidewalk and started to wave goodbye. At the last second, she sprinted back up the stairs and caught his sleeve.

"Would you mind if I cleaned up the gargoyles?" she asked. "Made them ready to be put back? I mean, if that's what you-all decide to do?"

The priest looked at her, surprised. "We don't have much money, Mary. And when we do hire people, we tend to hire from among the congregants."

"I don't want to be paid. I just want to make them look nice."

He frowned, looking back into the church as if there were answers there. "To tell the truth, none of the nuns want to go near the things. And I doubt the archdiocese will ever spring for the money to repair them. So...if you really want to do it, I'll find a way. But we have to keep it our little secret, if you don't mind."

"Then I'll see you next week at the same time?" she asked.

"You bet," he said. "Be prepared to get dirty, Mary Patronis. Those gargoyles have generations of pigeon poop on them."

Mary laughed and waved goodbye. As she walked down the sidewalk to the parking garage, she felt as if she was being watched. She looked up, and behind an old elm tree, she saw a small gargoyle she'd never noticed before. It was almost as if it was looking directly at her.

She nodded to the creature and turned away.

Chapter 4

The teasing started the moment Jon Williams showed up for work and didn't let up the whole day. It was only because he worked just two days a week that Jon could bear it at all.

It hadn't started out that way. The other workers hadn't known what to make of him. They'd be joshing each other, and Jon, not knowing how to join in, would stay quiet.

Finally, Kip Temple, who was the newest employee at the cathedral besides Jon, said, "You look like a teacher."

It was only after he agreed and told them of his plans that Jon realized the comment wasn't a compliment.

The next day, one of the others had said, "You look like an accountant."

Jon hadn't known what to say to that, so again, he'd kept quiet. After that, it was unrelenting.

"Hey, librarian!"

What wouldn't have been an insult coming from anyone else was an obvious belittlement when these guys said it.

Belittlement, Jon thought. *Yeah, use that word in their presence and I'll never hear the end of it.*

If the other guys were laughing and talking and he came within earshot, they'd fall silent. The message was pretty clear. He wasn't welcome.

"Hey, Jon," Ollie Simmons said to him one day. "I can't remember. If I wear an earring in my right ear, does that mean I'm a fag? Or is it my left ear?"

"I have no idea," Jon said amid their laughter.

One day when Kip and Jon were working together, the other man seemed almost friendly. "It isn't personal, Jon," he said confidingly. "You just shouldn't be here. You're taking a fucking job from some guy who needs it."

I *need it!* Jon wanted to shout, but he'd learned that the worst thing he could do was try to defend himself.

It didn't help when Hardy, the foreman, took him off the heavier jobs and gave him the task of cleaning up. They were short-handed. A couple of crews of six men each were barely able to keep up with the maintenance of the cathedral, much less make the repairs needed to keep it open. Father Michael was constantly raising money, but it seemed like very little of it was trickling down to the men actually doing the work.

After the gargoyle fell down and killed that man, the main task became to examine and, if necessary, to remove all the sculptures. Jon came along after the others removed the gargoyles. His job was to tidy up, to make it appear, if possible, that nothing was missing. It turned out he had a talent for that—probably something to do with his artistic instinct, the same thing that led him to his degree and the same thing that made him a target for the other workers. Jon learned that he could blend certain colors of brick and mortar to make it look like the holes were natural architectural features.

Still, the constant teasing—bullying, really—was wearing him down. Nothing he did worked. Teasing them back, laughing, scowling, fighting, ignoring them; he'd tried everything he could think of.

He couldn't quit his job. His financial aid depended on it. But if he got fired, the college would have to find him another job. One day, he brought the subject up with Hardy, who seemed dismayed at the idea.

"You're the only guy who can do the finer stuff," Hardy said. "I need you, Jon. Just ignore those other assholes. They don't really mean it."

"Yeah, they do mean it," Jon said.

19

"Well...maybe. But they're *assholes*. I'll tell you what. Why don't you just report to me? You can come in on your own time, stay away from the others. I'll tell you what needs to be done."

Jon hated to give up, but after a few days, it was clear that the new arrangement was an improvement. The other guys, when they saw him, seemed more curious about what he was doing than interested in continuing their bullying. Hardy, meanwhile, often accompanied Jon on his jobs, watching him, helping him out.

"I think I'll be doing this after you leave," Hardy said. "None of the others even understand what you're doing."

Jon had only a couple of weeks left when Kip failed to show up for work for a couple of days. Jon had to join the main crew, but for once, they left him alone. They seemed subdued, barely noticing he was there.

Kip was feeling a little guilty about the way he was treating Jon Williams. The guy wasn't really so bad one on one. It was just that he didn't seem to understand that the ragging was part of the deal, a rite of passage.

Certainly, Kip had been the brunt of it in the months before Jon had come along and become the new fish.

Jon should have just laughed and kept silent, but the guy was a loner—he'd probably never had a group of friends before. *Too bad; not my problem.*

Actually, Kip's real problem was with the other guys. They still weren't including him in their after-hours socializing, something Kip had been certain would happen once he ceased to be the "new guy." They went off together to some other room in the cathedral than their workroom, and they didn't invite him along. It was somewhere on the upper levels. He'd seen them stomping up the stairs, and once, when he'd tried to join them, they had all turned and looked at him like they didn't know him.

What the fuck?

He explored the upper levels on his own, and finally found a locked room on the same level as the storeroom where they were putting the gargoyles.

Why is it locked? he'd wondered. But there was no doubt, it had to be the place the other guys were going. So...he'd simply be there waiting for them.

He was standing there, looking at the door, when he sensed someone behind him. He jumped in alarm, and then felt a surge of relief when he saw that it was a priest. Kip had met Father Michael when he'd been hired and had seen him around the cathedral, but this priest was new. He was short and portly, but had a kindly face.

"You scared me, man," Kip said lamely.

"Pardon," the priest answered. "I wasn't expecting anyone."

"Yeah, well. My friends are coming up here, I think. But I don't have a key."

"No?" The priest raised his bushy eyebrows, then reached into his pocket and pulled out a huge keyring. "Let's see...I think it's this one."

The key was an enormous skeleton key; it looked ancient. Kip watched as the priest opened the huge door, suddenly feeling misgivings. He couldn't put his finger on what was wrong, but the door and the key and the priest all seemed so old-fashioned, as if Kip had traveled a hundred years into the past.

"Thanks," he said, pushing the door all the way open.

"You're very welcome, son," the priest said, nodding. He gathered up his robes and walked briskly away: from behind, it looked as if he was waddling. Kip almost burst out laughing.

So...should be some beer in here, he thought, looking for a light switch. He'd seen his coworkers boisterously descending the stairs after one of their sessions, completely soused. *I'll get a head start on them.*

Truth was, he was feeling a little shaky. What if they got mad at him? What if they told him to leave?

There wasn't an electric light that he could find. Kip held open the door, letting the dim light from the hallway filter into the room while

21

his eyes adjusted. There, on a broad table in the middle of the room, were some candles, with matches lying beside them. He gauged the distance to the matches and let the door close behind him. As his hand brushed across the surface of the rough, pitted table, covered with melted candle wax, and picked up the box of matches, he felt suddenly cold.

It had been a hot day outside, which was one of the reasons Kip had decided that today was the day to join his fellows in some cold drinks. But this chill was like the inside of a refrigerator, or as if he was hundreds of feet underground instead of two stories up in a cathedral. In fact, it had gotten warmer as he had ascended the stairs, he realized.

Not only was it cold in here, but a breeze blew across his face, and he felt his frown almost freeze into place.

Cold beer, he reminded himself. *There's a cold beer in this, if nothing else.*

Kip lit a match and the temperature immediately rose, and he shivered away the cold and felt sweat spring out all over his body.

He lit two of the candles and sat down on one of the stools that lined the table. Ten of them, he counted. Exactly the number of workers there were besides him and Jon Williams. As the candlelight flickered further into the darkness, a face lunged out at him and he cried out, nearly falling backward off the stool.

It was only a gargoyle: a big one, and a really ugly one. He'd never seen one in this style before, despite having seen every gargoyle on the cathedral. It must have been removed and stored here before he came to work.

There were other gargoyles in the room, farther back, and each of them appeared to have a unique shape. Kip had noticed that there seemed to be two types: the big gargoyles on the balustrades and the small gargoyles sprinkled throughout the cathedral. These gargoyles were of neither type, and looked as if they had been made individually instead of from molds; as if they were from an older time, when craftsmen were artists and created each feature of a cathedral by hand.

They appeared to be squirming, moving in and out of focus. Kip pulled one of the candles off the table, spilling hot wax on his hand as it broke away. He smothered a grunt of pain and stepped toward the phalanx of gargoyles.

The candlelight seemed to stop inches away from them, as if there was some kind of barrier between the creatures and the light. The cold returned, and Kip shivered. He leaned down to get a closer look at the nearest gargoyle.

It opened its red eyes. The gray stone burst into color, reds and yellows, and streaks of orange. It opened its mouth, revealing the long, sharp fangs of a demon and a huge, broad tongue emerged and licked Kip's face.

It all happened before he could move, and once the moisture on his face froze, he felt paralyzed. He fell backward, unable to stop his head from bouncing off the hard marble floor. The candle was snuffed out.

A roaring cold breeze washed over him, and the candle on the table also went out, and he was left in darkness.

"Kip didn't show up for work today," Hardy told Jon. "You'll have to take his place. We're checking the gargoyles on the east side of the cathedral, near the entrance."

"All right," Jon said. He looked at the others, expecting to see disgust. Instead, he got blank looks.

"I'll help you, since you haven't done removal before," Hardy said.

Chapter 5

As Mary walked away, the gargoyle yearned to fly after her, to beg her to return. A grinding noise came from beneath, almost as though he had really moved. An elm leaf, long stuck to his forehead, fell away and floated to the ground.

Mary turned the corner.

A man in a long black coat was following her. He appeared to be talking on his cellphone, but Dominic saw that he was watching Mary intently. She turned around as if sensing she was being watched (though whether by the man shadowing her or by Dominic, it was hard to know). The man didn't look threatening. He looked like a businessman deep in the throes of working out the details of a deal on the phone. Mary turned away.

She's in danger, Dominic thought. He didn't know how he knew this, but he did. It was part of why he was awake, why he was focused on this one woman. He was meant to save her.

Worry overwhelmed Dominic, for he was certain, as always, he'd never see her again. For two centuries, life had passed by him on the street below, fleeting and insubstantial. He'd barely noticed. Now, unexpectedly, the soft light of a gentle soul had entered his life. He was deathly afraid this new vivacity would be snuffed out without a thought, without him knowing, and he'd return to his nothingness, a creature as dull as his façade. It was up to him to save her, and he was helpless.

Time, which had passed unnoticed before, slowed like the raindrops falling on his head, dripping down his face, as slow as the erosion of his stone façade, as he waited for her return. Every passing storm, every bright sunny day seemed to last forever, an emptiness without Mary, meaningless except in anticipation.

Dominic never knew, when she left, whether she would ever come back to the cathedral. Her faith was weak, almost nonexistent, more a childhood memory of God than a real belief, a faith that had come from her parents' certainty and that had all but vanished when she'd finally broken away from them. Her visits to the cathedral were based on nostalgia and whim, and anything stronger that came into her life—another man, another job, anything substantial at all—could easily replace that wavering impulse.

She looked at me!

The gargoyle had tried, over the long years, to reach the humans passing below. He stared at them, of course—he could do nothing else if they were in his line of sight—but in addition, he concentrated furiously. *Look at me!* he'd think. *Look up!* Once in a great while, one would glance up briefly, as if bothered by a pesky fly. But the gargoyle had never been certain it wasn't simply coincidence.

She nodded to me!

"A falling leaf from the elm caught her attention," the ghost of Margerie Marcotte said lightly in his ear.

"Go away," he said.

"I wish only to save you from disappointment, dear Dominic," she said. Of all the ghosts, she was his most persistent tormentor. He'd watched her fall to her death, throwing herself and her unborn bastard child from the parapets, helpless to stop it, long before the elm tree had been planted. Indeed, one of the trees was a memorial to her, planted by her sisters.

The unborn child had passed on, a bright light shooting into the sky, into whatever heaven existed. But Margerie had stayed behind, unwilling to forgive herself, and even more unwilling to forgive the man who had betrayed her. That man was long dead, but any man served in his stead for her wrath. Even a man who'd been turned into a stone gargoyle, unable to ever tempt a woman again.

"Leave him alone!" Alastair Hamilton shouted. A cuckolded husband had killed the banker on the very steps of the cathedral. "In God's house, with Him as my witness, to be certain you go to hell!" the man had exclaimed as he fired the fatal shot.

"Witless man," Margerie said. "You have no idea what Dominic is feeling. You never felt as he feels now."

That seemed to surprise both Alastair and Dominic. Had Margerie just defended the gargoyle?

"He's lost in a pathetic illusion," she continued. "I merely point out the truth."

"Ah, thank God you're here to enlighten us," Alastair said. "Otherwise, how would we ever know the truth?"

"Thank God?" she sneered. "Are you finally willing to face His judgment?'

"A turn of phrase," Alastair muttered.

Dominic tried to ignore the bickering ghosts. Which was difficult, for they stood in the air before his eyes, as firmly as if standing on the sidewalk below. He saw them in human form, with the branches of the elms weaving seamlessly through their incorporeal bodies. Alistair Hamilton was dressed in the height of early 1900s fashion, complete with a top hat and a black tie, while Margerie Marcotte was dressed in a maid's uniform from the same era.

It was doubtless no accident they had found each other. They were two foes locked in an unending battle. Their feud had probably kept them anchored as ghosts to the cathedral, whereas alone, each might possibly have "given up the ghost" and moved on. Unfortunately for Dominic, they tended to linger near his perch, as if asking him to be the judge of their arguments. He was careful to never express an opinion, but it didn't seem to matter. They seemed to be able to read his thoughts anyway.

A human voice drifted down to them, and Alastair and Margerie disappeared. Most humans couldn't see ghosts, but they tended to avoid contact nevertheless. Dominic suspected living humans reminded the ghosts too much of their past, and even more of their present, and worst of all, led to thoughts about the future they had long resisted. Either way, it put an end to their hauntings.

He heard the humans coming down the side of the cathedral from above. It was too early for routine cleaning, which cycled around to this part of the building every decade or so. The repairs were coming closer, but were probably still years away. Ropes came swinging down in front of his eyes, swaying from the motion of the men descending.

Dominic felt a heavy boot scuff up against his right horn. Once upon a time, the point of the horn might have penetrated the leather sole, but erosion had long since dulled the point, just as it had faded all his features. He had wide, glaring eyes, which once upon a time had looked as though they were peering into onlookers' souls, heavy brows, and a gaping mouth with the tongue hanging down. The tongue had once been twice as long, tapering to a point, but it had been broken off long ago, the victim of a careless cleaner. The gargoyles on this side of the building got little attention, and in earlier times had been avoided by most of the workers.

Dominic was crouched over on massive, taloned feet, and once it had looked as if he was preparing to leap into the air at any moment. Somehow, over the years, that predatory leap had slowly become less aggressive, as if he was exhausted by the eternal promise of flight. Now he didn't so much look prepared to leap forward as to settle back onto his hindquarters. He was a blurred version of his once-frightening self.

"Hey, boss," the man directly above him shouted. "Come look at this!"

A second set of boots descended next to him, and Dominic could see dusty leather and frayed shoelaces out of the corner of his eye.

"What?" the second voice said after a moment. "I don't see anything."

"Look at the base of this thing," the first man said. "See all that broken concrete? It looks like the statue is coming loose."

"Huh," the boss said, sounding only half interested. "Wonder what caused that? Well, we better take it off, just to be on the safe side. The holy fathers have been wanting us to either clean or remove these buggers for a long time." The man's voice sounded disparaging when he used the words "holy fathers." "Got your chisel, Freddy?"

"Yeah," the man said.

"I'll swing a basket down," the boss said, his voice receding as he ascended back up the ropes.

The "basket" was really a heavy canvas bag. An overwhelming sense of vertigo came over Dominic as he was broken away from his long imprisonment. For the first time since his transformation, his line of vision was upended. For two centuries, he'd seen only the part of the world that was directly in front of him; now the blue sky tilted above him, the ground looked as if it was falling toward him, and the branches of the trees appeared to be trying to stab him.

A sense of loss overcame him. He'd wanted nothing more than to get away from his long captivity, and yet—it had been safe, predictable, and now as he was removed, he felt panic and uncertainty.

The worker struggled to fit the gargoyle into the mouth of the bag, at one point shouting to passersby below to get across the street. Men in overalls came around the side of the cathedral and put up ropes around the elm trees to keep pedestrians away. Bits of concrete showered down, and dust coated the base of the elms with a gray powder.

At first, Dominic didn't so much feel the man's touch as sense his nearness. The workman's glove slipped while he was trying to lift the gargoyle up.

"Hell with it," the man muttered. Then the gargoyle felt the bare hands of the man taking a firmer hold and lifting him away from the building, tipping him upside down.

Then the canvas bag closed over him, and he was plunged into darkness.

But in those few moments of contact, an entire new life had entered his mind, and Dominic realized that it wasn't just Mary Patronis that he could understand and feel, but this young man as well.

Let go of me! he shouted out in his mind.

The man nearly dropped him, crying out in surprise.

Chapter 6

L et go of me!

The words were clear as day, and Jon almost dropped the bag, which he hadn't yet attached to the rope. If he'd lost hold of it, it would have landed on the sidewalk below, shattering into pieces near one of the elm trees.

He'd been admiring the gargoyle, and so apparently his imagination had decided to personify the creature. *Appreciation is one thing*, he thought, *but this is crazy.*

Jon wrestled the gargoyle into the canvas bag, trying to ignore the feeling that the thing was alive. He could swear that it had been warm to the touch, and that there was a rhythmic pulse to its surface.

Hardy would laugh at such an observation. To him, Jon was the college boy foisted upon him by the priests. He seemed to be warming up to his subordinate, but slowly, so slowly that anyone watching would never catch it at all.

As Jon closed the bag over the base of the gargoyle, he noticed faint numbers on it. He hesitated. He'd never seen that before. He'd come up with his own numbering system for keeping track of the statues, and it made sense that whoever had put the gargoyles into place had also had a system.

W3–1, it said. *W for west*, Jon guessed. *3 for being on the third level. 1 for being the first gargoyle from the entrance on that level.* He couldn't remember exactly, but it seemed as if this was the same numbering system Jon had devised.

Jon pulled himself up the roof with the canvas bag trailing below him on a line, making sure the bulky package didn't swing against the wall and especially that it got nowhere near the stained-glass windows. The gargoyle really hadn't been that heavy, considering it was solid stone, but it had been an awkward weight. Mostly it had been Hardy watching him that had made Jon so clumsy.

It was the first time Hardy had let Jon detach one of the gargoyles. Since Richard Song had called in sick, he'd had little choice.

"It's a small one," Hardy had said. "May as well learn sometime."

Jon knew Hardy thought his job should go to a deserving unemployed construction worker, not some college art history student who wouldn't ever use the skills taught to him again. Jon had often wanted to tell his boss that it was because he was an art student that he needed to know these skills. There weren't a lot of jobs for what he was learning. Jon thought that having some practical skills might make all the difference in his ambitions.

But he also thought any defensiveness on his part would only make it worse. Besides, he had to admit that the only reason he had the job was because his professors had insisted.

It was all worth it. Just to be around this magnificent cathedral for twenty hours a week was worth all the hazing, all the teasing the other workers gave him. Halfway through the year, Jon had even considered switching his major to architecture, then had realized that learning how a cathedral was built was probably even more useless than art history. *Not a lot of cathedrals being built these days*, he'd thought.

When he'd first arrived, he'd announced grandly that when he was done with his internship here, he was going to get a job at the Sagrada Familia cathedral in Barcelona. To his surprise, Hardy had known what he was talking about.

"From what I've heard, learning construction would be more helpful to you than art," Hardy had said. Jon had to admit he was right, and had set about learning all he could from the older man. Sure enough, he'd been hired—the Sagrada Foundation was looking for all the help they could get—and it had been Jon's work at the cathedral more than his art studies that had gotten him the job.

Jon pulled himself onto the roof and detached his gear. He leaned over the side of the balustrade and pulled the bag the rest of the way up. Jon had filled out over the past year, his shoulders broadening, new muscles developing in his arms and legs, until he barely recognized himself. He no longer looked like a geeky kid. Some of the newer female undergrads had started flirting with him, but since he was practically on his way to Spain, he saw little point in following through.

"Following through?" Hardy had laughed when Jon made the mistake of turning down a date in front of his boss. "Is that what you call it? I call it a fucking one-night stand."

Hardy was a gruff middle-aged guy who, and though he was healthy for his age, had started letting Richard and Jon do most of the physical work. Jon had the sense the older man had become fond of him, or if not fond, at least defended him to the other workers when he wasn't around.

"Leave him be," Jon had heard him say. "He's paid his dues."

Again, an outsider might not have noticed any letup of the ribbing Jon got, but the tone had changed from mean to affectionate in Jon's ears.

He turned to see if Hardy was watching, but his boss was already heading inside. Jon hurried to follow, since he didn't know where the gargoyles were stored.

Hardy was waiting for him at the door, and motioned him to follow. Jon slung the bag with the gargoyle in it over his shoulder. The older man descended about halfway down the spiral staircase before turning aside on a floor that Jon had barely been aware of and that he'd never actually explored. The gargoyle's broken tongue was starting to gouge into Jon's back, and he readjusted it.

To his surprise, there was a series of storerooms on this floor, mostly filled with old construction material that, from the looks of it, would never be used. The modern materials held up better and came in more convenient packaging. The priests would probably just let this stuff rot here forever, since it would be too much trouble to remove it.

Jon had noticed a lot of empty spaces where statues had once stood, and he had assumed they'd been lost to the damage of time. In fact, it had been one of his midterm projects to document the remaining gargoyles with photos and a map of their location. The cathedral was always short of money for repairs, which—since the college paid half his wages—was one of the reasons Jon had been hired. The two small crews of workmen, which consisted of Hardy and Jon and usually—though he was sick this day—Richard Song during the daytime and another couple of men in the evenings, were hardly keeping up.

"Fight the entropy," Hardy often said as they started the day. "Am I using that word right, college boy?"

"I know what you mean," Jon offered. "But I think we're losing."

"We always lose in the end," Hardy said matter of factly. "Gravity always triumphs...or 'grabbity,' as my daughter Sarah used to say when she was younger."

At the end of the hall was the biggest of the rooms, and when Jon entered, he was stunned. It was filled with gargoyles, big and small. Some were beaten-up and ugly, others were almost handsome, but all of them were neglected, littering the floor as if they had been tossed there.

"They're beautiful," Jon breathed.

His boss rolled his eyes, and Jon knew that if Richard had been at work that day, he would never have heard the end of the teasing. He didn't care. Sometimes beauty was beauty.

"They're ugly fuckers and a pain in the ass to clean," Hardy said. "Medieval bullshit."

Jon decided not to push his luck. "Where do I put this one?" he asked.

"Just...anywhere. By the door, that will be fine."

Jon gingerly lowered the bag and felt the tension in his shoulders release. The gargoyle was heavier than it had appeared at first. Trying not to show any weakness, Jon lifted the gargoyle out of the bag, using his gloves this time. He placed it on the floor.

I never knew these gargoyles were here, he thought. *I need to study them.*

Jon had thought he'd documented all the gargoyles, but here was a whole new batch of them.

"Do you mind if I stay for a few minutes?" he asked Hardy.

"Stay all you want," Hardy shrugged. "Your shift is done. You've got another couple of shifts next week, but to tell you the truth, you don't really need to show up. You've done a good job, Jon. I'm glad to have met you." He extended his big, beefy hand and Jon took it, surprised at his boss's warm tone.

"Thank you, sir. It has been a great experience."

"Well...good. I wish you luck in your career, young man." The older man started looking uncomfortable, as if wondering if he'd gone too far in his friendliness. He turned abruptly and left the room.

Jon pulled off his glove and put his hand on top of the gargoyle. It was encrusted with bird dung, but Jon had seen worse.

A shock of recognition passed through him. He stared into the gargoyle's eyes, and it was as if the gargoyle was staring back. Jon had had that impression before when examining some of the Old Masters' paintings, as if the creators were still there somehow, but never so strongly as this.

At least the gargoyle didn't speak to him this time.

Jon pulled his notebook out of his back pocket and got to work. The biggest gargoyle was directly across the room. It was so heavy he could barely tip it onto its side, and almost dropped it when the heavier front swung around. Sure enough, there were numbers there, though written in a different color and a different hand. Made sense. The bigger gargoyles had been made more than a hundred years later than the smaller ones.

The numbers were on the bottoms of the gargoyles' bases, and the paint was hard to read. Jon marked the numbers down in his notebook, describing the size and function of the gargoyle, then went through the rest of the room. In places, he had to guess what the numbers were: there were sevens that looked a lot like twos, threes that could just as easily be fives. He'd sort it all out later.

"What are you doing here?" he heard a loud voice say.

Jon's heart fell when he saw the tall, skeletal figure dressed in black at the door. "Stay away from Father Michael," Hardy had told him after Jon was hired. "Let me deal with him. I know just what suck-up things to say."

Now Jon stuttered, "I'm...ah...writing down the numbers on the gargoyles."

"Why on earth are you doing that?"

"I'm a graduate student in art history" Jon said. "That's why I was given this job." The tall priest stared at him, and Jon realized he'd made a mistake. The priest had been the one who'd given the OK for his hire. "Jon Williams," he said.

"Oh, yes. I remember now," the priest said. "I don't know why you're bothering. If it was up to me, I'd scrap these ugly monstrosities."

Jon was horrified by the thought, but he didn't object, prudently managing to merely nod.

"Well, finish up and go home. We aren't paying you for overtime." The priest left without waiting for a response.

Jon had only the little gargoyle he'd removed that day left to look at. He remembered the numbers, W4-1, and yet for some reason felt insecure about his memory. He turned the gargoyle over.

Don't touch me!

Jon nearly dropped the gargoyle. The broken tongue caught his palm and sliced into it, and blood flowed down his wrist and dripped into the creature's mouth.

"Shit!" he exclaimed, dropping the gargoyle so that it fell on its side. He contemplated picking it up again, and then snorted. *Leave it be. Go put some disinfectant on the cut.*

"I'll see you again, little fella," he said, and laughed at the vividness of his own imagination. The gargoyle had to be a couple of hundred years old, and yet here he was feeling protective of it. "Don't go anywhere."

Chapter 7

D^{*on't touch me!*}

Don't touch me!
Dominic was stunned that the human had read his thought. He was even more dumbfounded when the man's blood flowed over him and a flood of strange emotions and memories flashed into his mind.

He almost retreated into the somnolent state in which he'd spent most of his existence, the dead stone where there were no feelings or thoughts. It was all too much—being uprooted from his perch, twirled upside down, and stuffed into darkness. But worse was the intrusion of another consciousness flooding his mind. He was still reeling from that brief glimpse of another soul.

He had thought his connection to Mary was special, and yet here were another human's feelings and desires invading his world. It had only been a moment, but in that brief contact, it was as if Jon Williams's entire history had been illuminated.

Jon had patted him on the head, and Dominic could sense that the man was dismissing their connection as an illusion. Dominic was careful this time to keep his mind blank.

Then he was left alone—or so he thought. He heard a guttural muttering from somewhere else in the room. He still felt a sense of vertigo, despite not moving, because for the first time in a long time, he was seeing something other than the view down the long boulevard. He couldn't quite adjust to the short distance before him, and he couldn't make sense of the clutter around him.

"Someone new, praise the saints," he heard a harsh voice say. From the corner of one eye, he could see the gnarled claws of another gargoyle. From the size of the talons, it was one of the bigger gargoyles with waterspouts that lined the upper buttresses.

"Hello?" Dominic said. "Where am I?"

"If you thought you were in purgatory before," the harsh voice said, "you're in hell now."

Another, feminine-sounding voice came from a part of the room Dominic couldn't see. "No, just more purgatory. At least you're out of the rain."

"I *liked* the rain," said the harsher voice. "I *liked* my job."

"That's because you are a dimwit who's good for nothing but gargling on rainwater." Dominic couldn't see the other gargoyle, but from the tone and volume of the voice, he suspected that the speaker was small and delicate.

"And you are nothing more than a pretty decoration."

"Pretty?" the second, softer voice sounded amused. "I suppose compared to you I am. Technically, I am not a gargoyle at all, since my purpose was not to divert the water but, as you say, simply to be a decoration. I am called a chimera, or—and you should pay particular attention to this, Mr. Grotesque—a Boss."

"You are nothing but a lump of stone now, Pretty, just like the rest of us," the harsher voice said.

"Sadly true," the softer voice agreed. "Modern humans do not believe we ward off evil anymore. They don't think we protect the cathedral. We must pray they come to their senses before it is too late."

"They still need *us*," the larger gargoyle said. "Those of us on the buttresses still serve a purpose."

"Perhaps. From the Latin *gurgulio*, you serve as a 'throat,' or a simple gutter. But a long piece of tubing can do the same job without the upkeep. Humans don't care if their waterspouts have faces anymore."

"Please," Dominic finally interrupted. "Why am I here? What has happened?"

Pretty answered. "You're here to be repaired and restored and returned to your perch…though as far as I know, that has yet to happen to any of us. I've been here the longest, I believe. I was always inside, a 'decoration,' as Grotesque says, placed over the entrance to the library. During the earthquake of 1869, I became loose. A monk took me down and stored me here. Since then, a menagerie of our fellows has joined me, though most of these unfortunates have long ago fallen silent. Dead, I suppose."

"They probably just got tired of listening to you," Grotesque said.

"Certainly, I am glad to have someone else to talk to. You have nothing interesting to say, Grotesque. I don't know why you are still alive."

"Perhaps I stay awake just to spite you, Pretty."

Dominic had a feeling that this argument had been going on for a very long time, and that it was going to become tiresome very fast.

"Please," he said. "I don't understand any of this."

The two bickering gargoyles fell silent.

"Forgive us," Grotesque's rumbling voice said after a spell. "I remember how disorienting it was when I first got here."

"Yes, you must pardon us," said Pretty. "We have tried to retain our sanity through our silly arguments. I forgot how it might sound to a newcomer."

"There have been others who were awake?" Dominic asked.

Again, there was a long silence.

"For a time," Pretty said quietly. "But they all stopped talking, eventually. It's understandable. We have lost our purpose, have we not? Perhaps falling into silence is the proper response and Grotesque and I are the deluded ones."

"Pretty thinks she's smart because she decorated the entrance to a library," Grotesque confided. "As if it was she who read the books."

"I listened to many a long discourse," Pretty said. "I learned more than any of the students. However, I fear with only Grotesque to talk to, my brain has withered. I so hope you have some wits..." Pretty hesitated. "What is your name?"

"Dominic," the gargoyle answered.

"Dominic? You have a human name?"

"I was once human."

This time, the silence was so long and so deep that Dominic was afraid that Pretty and Grotesque had retreated into the same dumb state as the rest of the gargoyles in the storeroom.

Pretty finally broke the silence. "I heard them talk of you, though the monks thought you were a legend. Nobody could remember which of the chimeras you were supposed to be. You were lost."

"I was always where I was," Dominic answered.

"Just so," Grotesque rumbled. "I was always meant to be what I am…a rain gutter. Pretty here was always meant to be merely an adornment, despite her air of superiority. Yet even though we were created to be silent and still, it has been hard to endure. I can only imagine how it must be for you, Dominic."

Dominic didn't know what to say to that. Up to that moment, he hadn't really been afraid: disoriented and confused, perhaps, but not frightened. Now, as he stared at the slate floor and the small glimpse of Grotesque's claws, the implications began to sink in. He'd always had a view of the city that, while narrow, had been long and busy. He'd always been able to watch the humans passing by. The weather and the light were always changing.

Now, he was locked in a small room without a view, and while he had company, they had clearly gone insane from their imprisonment.

Worst of all, he'd never see *her* again. *She'll never even know that I'm gone.*

And then, almost as if in response to his thought, Mary Patronis walked in the door.

Chapter 8

Father Gregory couldn't conceal his surprise when Mary actually showed up the following week. He seemed annoyed and pleased at the same time: annoyed to have to think about the gargoyles, yet pleased someone was finally tackling the problem.

"They're filthy," he said. "Be careful...there's years of guano on them."

Mary drew plastic gloves out of her backpack and brandished them. "I'm prepared. I'm guano take care of the problem."

Father Gregory groaned at the pun.

"All right," he said doubtfully. "If you really mean it. But I won't blame you if you find it too much. Do as much or as little as you please. To tell you the truth, I'm not completely sure these gargoyles will ever be reinstalled."

Mary was dressed even more casually than usual, having dug her oldest clothes out of the back of the closet, a strange combination of a worn dress blouse and some old gym pants. She didn't figure anyone was going to see her.

Father Gregory led her up the spiral stairs. About halfway up, there was a small bathroom. "You can get your water from here," he said. "Pour the dirty water into the toilet, if you will. The sink has old plumbing that clogs up easily."

There was a small utility closet on the same floor as the storeroom where the gargoyles were stowed, and inside, Mary found brushes and pails. It was obvious they hadn't been used in a long time. There was a bag of powdered soap, and she quickly realized that it was so concentrated that she needed to use only a little in each pail full of water.

She stood at the doorway of the storeroom, the steaming pail in one hand, a stiff brush in the other, and stared at the gargoyles, paralyzed by their size and number.

What have I gotten myself into? she asked herself.

The largest gargoyles were toward the back, leaning against the wall just under the window. The glass was filthy, and the glow of the morning sun barely lit the room. She looked around for a light switch, found one, and flipped it, but when the bare bulb in the ceiling came on, it didn't add appreciably to the light.

Near the door were some smaller gargoyles, which had apparently been added to the collection later. Mary recognized them as coming from the side of the cathedral rather than the balustrades.

I'll start with the easier ones.

A small gargoyle lay on its side, just inside the door. It was about half her size, and she was able to wrestle it upright. It looked vaguely familiar, though she couldn't imagine why.

This is the one, she thought, looking into its eyes. The stone felt almost warm to the touch. Despite the glaring eyes, the horns, and the gaping jaws, the creature didn't look malevolent; it seemed almost thoughtful, as if it had started out angry, full of hate, and had wearied of it, had reconciled with its fate, and was at peace. She dipped the brush into the water and started on the top of the gargoyle's head, between the horns. The dirt and grime and guano at first seemed as hard at the rock itself, but as the moisture seeped in, it started to break apart in chunks. A big piece slid off, leaving a trail through the dust of the gargoyle's face. Underneath, the original stone surface was revealed.

The rock had an almost pearlescent shine, and the gray was mixed with streaks of red. Suddenly, this task seemed worthwhile. Mary wanted to see what this fellow really looked like underneath all the shit. She pushed down harder with the brush and more chunks came off, and it was as if a bird was hatching from an egg. The gargoyle's eyes were shinier than the surrounding rock, as if they had been polished. It gave the appearance that there was a soul beneath, staring out, pleased with her efforts.

She learned that if she splashed water on the gunk and let it sit for a while, it would loosen it up, making it easier to remove. It was messy, but she didn't think anyone would care. The water couldn't harm the slate floor, and she could sweep up the dirt when it all dried. Mary had cleaned most of the gargoyle's head when her cellphone rang.

For a moment, she couldn't figure out what it was. It was as if she had somehow been living in the past, in a time before there were such things as phones—when rock and water and air were the principal elements of everyday life.

Her phone was in her backpack. She rose with a groan, realizing that she'd been hunched over for so long that her muscles had cramped. She hurriedly peeled off her gloves, but by the time she had removed them, the phone had stop ringing.

She felt a sudden dread. Was she supposed to be at work today? She checked the number. Sure enough, it was her boss. With great reluctance, she decided she'd better call him back.

"Mr. Sutherland?" she said, when a gruff voice answered. "Did you need something?"

"Where the fuck are you?" he asked.

"It's...it's my day off, sir. I am volunteering at the church."

There was a long silence at this. "I didn't know you were religious," he said finally, as if grudgingly admitting that this might actually be an excuse he couldn't bully her out of.

"Is there something I can help you with?" she asked.

"Where the fuck did you put the Peterson papers? He wants the deal done...like yesterday."

"I put them on your desk before I left last night. All they need is your signature."

"Oh."

"I'll be back first thing tomorrow, sir," she said.

"Okay, I found them," he grunted. Then he asked what he had probably really called her to ask in the first place. "How did Peterson sound? Was he...pleased?"

Mary knew what he was asking. On a good day, Peterson sounded like he wanted to chop your head off; on a bad day, like he wanted to flay your skin off first. Mary had sympathy for her boss. She knew that the rest of the staff thought Sutherland was a complete bastard, but she tried to imagine herself in his position, having to deal every day with the likes of that billionaire prick Gerald Peterson. It would turn anyone into a cranky SOB.

"He sounded…normal," she answered. In other words, he sounded like an utter asshole, but no more so than usual.

"Good," Sutherland said, his relief obvious, though he was trying to sound casual. "That's good. I'll see you in the morning, then!" He hung up without waiting for an answer.

Mary clicked off the phone and dropped it into her bag. She turned, starting to put on the gloves again, then hesitated.

The gargoyle was looking at her. Well, of course he was. He couldn't help but look at her, facing directly toward her as he was. Yet…there seemed to be intelligence behind that look, and not only intelligence, but emotion, as if the gargoyle was somehow concerned for her, sympathetic to her plight.

"Only one more month, then I quit," she said to the gargoyle. "I swear."

The gargoyle appeared to blink in sympathy.

Mary closed her eyes and swayed, dizzy. *I've been working too hard,* she thought. *I'm starting to see things.* When she opened her eyes, the gargoyle was stone again, and yet the eerie sense of consciousness was still there.

"Look, it's not my fault that they are ripping people off," she told it. "I'm just the secretary. If it wasn't me doing my job, it would be someone else."

You are part of the sin when you ignore the sin, the gargoyle said.

"Okay, that's it," she said. "Just as soon as I finish you off, and I'm going to turn your face to the wall, you judgmental little beast. Then I'm done for the day."

Again she reached for the gloves, and again she hesitated. She reached out with her bare hand and rubbed the top of the gargoyle's head.

She sprang back with a cry, for it had felt as though the stone had gone soft, like skin, and that it had moved, almost as if there was a living pulse underneath it. *It is just anthropomorphism!* she thought in alarm. *Hell, you named your damn car Sylvester. No wonder you think a gargoyle is alive!*

She finished cleaning the statue, careful not to look into its eyes again. When she was done, she stood back and examined it.

It was beautiful. There was no other word for it. What had seemed vaguely creepy and threatening covered in soot and grime was exposed to be a tortured creature, not an evil one: a creature struggling with its demonic nature, the very essence of guilt and shame.

No wonder I relate to it.

She heard a voice from the doorway.

"I never knew…" Father Gregory stood frozen, as if stunned by the sight of the newly cleaned and—strange as it was to think it—beautiful gargoyle.

"Yeah," she agreed. "Who knew?"

Father Gregory finally approached the creature and bent down to look into its eyes.

"I think the congregation is wrong," he said. "These creatures must to be restored and returned to their proper places. They are the soul of the cathedral." He stood and beamed at her.

"Thank you so much for this blessing, Mary Patronis," he said.

"I'm glad to do it," she said. But inside, she was wishing she could back out of it. "The soul of the cathedral," the Father had said, and she thought he was right. At the very least, these gargoyles had the power to expose the souls of those who looked on them.

Just one more month, she thought. *Then I quit that job and never look back.*

Chapter 9

"She looked at you," Grotesque said with an awed tone. "She bent down and looked you right in the eye. I swear! And she patted you on the head."

"Of course she looked at him," Pretty said. "He's hard to miss."

"No, Pretty. You couldn't see from your angle, but she really *looked* at him, as if she saw him, as if she realized she was talking to a living soul."

"She just sounded crazy to me," Pretty said.

Mary had repositioned Dominic upright, so that he was now facing into the room. He could see most of the other gargoyles. Directly across from him was Grotesque.

Grotesque earned his name. His ears were bigger than most, and pointed, and his eyes were slanted, giving him an evil look. His tongue was forked, and his nose was as sharp as a knife. Pretty was positioned facing the corner, and Dominic could only see a small part of her, but what he could see told him that the name Pretty was an exaggeration. She had smaller features than most gargoyles, perhaps; her mouth was closed, and she didn't have horns; but her nose was huge and bulbous, and her forehead protruded.

Of the other gargoyles littering the room, most were dead, but a few appeared to be sleeping. All of them were damaged in some way, missing an ear or a horn, with a claw broken away, or crumbling about the base, and a thick coating of dust covered all of them. All but Dominic.

Outside the opaque window, the sky had grown dark, though it was midmorning. Thunder rumbled through the cathedral as it was shaken by the winds of the storm. Dominic had never minded the rain or snow or the heat of the sun, but now that he was out of the weather, he realized that he felt comfortable and secure.

"She saw him, Pretty," Grotesque repeated. "She looked right at him and spoke to him."

"I heard," Pretty answered. "But it sounded like she was talking to herself."

"I'm right, aren't I?" Grotesque demanded of Dominic. His eyes appeared to almost glow in the dimly lit room.

"Her name is Mary," Dominic said softly.

The other two gargoyles became still. Which was strange, because they hadn't been moving, at least not to mortal eyes. But to Dominic's eyes, it had seemed they were quivering in anticipation.

He told them about how Mary Patronis had visited the roof above, where Dominic was perched. How her boyfriend had followed her up there and had struck her, and how a single drop of blood had landed on Dominic's head.

"A single drop," Grotesque said. "And look at you. You look almost ready to fly."

Pretty didn't say anything, but Dominic sensed she wanted to. He waited. Rain lashed against the window, waves of windswept raindrops that managed to squeeze through the ancient window frames, trickling down the side of the wall and collecting in a puddle at Pretty's feet.

"You say you never knew her before?" Pretty asked, finally.

"How could I? I have been frozen on the side of this cathedral from the time it was built."

Again there was a long silence as his two new friends absorbed this information. "You are the oldest of us," Pretty said. "And yet you are still conscious."

"I had the ghosts to talk to," Dominic explained. "They lingered for years, some of them, and I learned much from them. What I saw from my perch sometimes seemed a blur, but the ghosts explained what I was seeing."

Neither Grotesque or Pretty said anything for a moment, and Dominic sensed he'd said something wrong.

"Ghosts?" Grotesque said skeptically. "I don't believe in ghosts."

"I've wondered," Pretty said, a little more thoughtfully. "I could swear sometimes that I heard spirits talking. I assumed some of the quiet gargoyles were dreaming."

Grotesque whistled. Dominic was looking right at him, and of course his features didn't change, but the sound of the whistle was clear and unmistakable. "I can't imagine the agony of what you've been through, Dominic. Pretty and me and all these others, we were made of stone; we can only imagine what it must be like to move freely. And yet, most of us haven't been able to endure even this. We have retreated into silent oblivion. But you...you who were once human and free, unable to move or speak for decades...it must have been unspeakable torture."

"I deserved it," Dominic said. "For most of that time, I was as these others you see, barely aware of my surroundings.

"No," Pretty said. "Whatever you did, no creature deserves such a fate." The gargoyle appeared to be staring down at the puddle of rainwater at the base of her claws as if in thought, though that was, of course, an illusion. All the movement, all the voices, were in Dominic's head. He wondered if he was making them up, but then...where did such thoughts come from, and how could he himself exist?"

"Hell of a coincidence," Grotesque said. "Her showing up like that."

"Not coincidence, but fate," Pretty said. "Dominic did not know this woman, and yet she arrives in this very room, a room that few humans have visited in the decades I've been here. Of all the gargoyles here, she picks you to clean first. This cannot be a coincidence."

Before Dominic could take in what Pretty was saying, Grotesque was laughing. "Or it's just a coincidence. I don't believe in fate."

"So says the talking gargoyle," Pretty retorted. "You can't believe how happy I am that you have showed up, Dominic. I have been arguing with this idiot for far too long. He believes in science and yet himself is a refutation of everything scientific. He can't accept the fact that were created to drive away demons."

46

Grotesque snorted. "There are no such things as demons."

"Seeeee…" Pretty said, drawing out the word. "It works!"

"Our consciousness is easy enough to explain," Grotesque said. "We don't exist. We are someone's dream."

If Pretty could have rolled her eyes, she would have done so. "Don't listen to him, Dominic. I think, perhaps, that your deliverance is at hand."

Dominic had not allowed himself to think it, but of course from the moment Mary had walked into the room, he'd realized that the possibility existed.

Grotesque saved him from answering. "Well, I suppose the woman could cut her throat and drain her blood over Dominic. That might do it."

"I don't believe it was her blood that woke Dominic," Pretty said. "It was merely the instrument that connected them. Something else is happening, and you and me, Grotesque, have the privilege of watching." Pretty laughed, a strangely feminine little trill coming as it did from a lump of stone facing the corner.

Grotesque's rumbling laughter joined hers. "I *knew* there was a reason I stayed awake. Because it sure as hell wasn't because I enjoyed talking to you."

Dominic had never thought that the curse could be lifted. It was impossible. He had been frozen in stone on the side of a cathedral, unable to move or speak in a way that any mortal could apprehend. How could he ever be freed from that fate?

Even when he'd come awake with Mary's drop of blood, he'd known that the love could be only one-sided, that he could yearn to be with her, but she would never know it.

The monk who had cursed him to take this shape had been very clear: "Until you love someone more than you love yourself, you shall be damned to eternal silence."

Chapter 10

Mary made her way down the stairs to Father Gregory's office. The cathedral was becoming familiar to her, but her sense of awe and reverence remained. She was starting to notice the little details. There were sculptures and frescoes throughout the building, inside as well as outside. The carvings inside tended to be smaller and more decorative than the ones outside, but still alien to the modern world. Many supernatural creatures were depicted in those frescoes, and Mary remembered reading about how the Catholic Church had been adept, in its early years, at appropriating other cultures' and religions' symbols and myths for their own use.

The small vault that Father Gregory occupied would probably appear bare and medieval without the tapestries and pictures, the soft couch along one side, the large oriental rug, and the long, cluttered desk. As it was, it looked more like a home office than one inside a centuries-old structure. Bare stone was visible only in small nooks and crannies, in the inches between pictures, and at the edges of the rug.

Father Gregory had his head down, reading some papers in his lap. Mary knocked gently. He looked up, and for a few moments it was clear to Mary that he didn't remember who she was. Then his face broke out into a wide smile, and he pushed his chair away from the desk and stood.

"Mary! Is it that time of week again already?"

"I'm a day early, Father. I thought I should check in."

"That's thoughtful of you, but you don't need to do that," he said. "You can go straight up."

She smiled back and turned to leave.

"It's interesting you should show up," he said, causing her to turn back around. "I was just studying the budget, trying to find some money to put the gargoyles back. It turns out it's an expensive process because of the safety concerns. All kinds of regulations. It might have been better never to remove them, because they were grandfathered in. Now…well, it's an issue."

Mary came all the way back into the office and stood in front of his desk. "Perhaps we could raise the money through benefits and fundraisers," she said.

"Even that might be more political than you think," Father Gregory said. "I'm not in charge of repairs, which means I have no say over the gargoyles. That is Father Michael's duty, and frankly, between you and me, I don't think he cares much. We have fundraisers every week, or so it seems. People are fighting for their own pet projects to be included. Gargoyles aren't on anyone's list."

"Except for ours," she said.

He looked surprised, then nodded. "Yes, except for ours. So we're going to have to find a way on our own, I suspect."

"Well, I'll clean them, at least."

"That's a start," Father Gregory said, looking down at the papers on the desk. "I know a couple of rich benefactors who are interested in the arts. Perhaps if I present this as a cultural issue, they might come through with a donation. But as I said, the board might look askance at that priority."

"What if it was the benefactors' idea?" she asked. "If the board believes that the money is coming from the outside, I doubt they'll reject it."

Father Gregory smiled slyly. "I see you have a devious mind. Three Hail Marys and a little more of that, if you please."

"Hail Mary, full of grace…" Mary began. "That's about as much as I know."

"You were a Catholic in a past life, I just know it."

"A priest who believes in reincarnation?"

"I'll deny it if you tell anyone else, but I believe in almost everything. I've seen things in this cathedral that can't be explained by Church doctrine."

Is he talking about the gargoyles? Mary wondered. She couldn't shake the feeling that the gargoyle she'd been cleaning had been almost alive, or that other gargoyles in the room had been watching her. She'd even imagined that she heard their thoughts.

The gargoyle she'd started with had seemed to be completely in love with her, almost as if he knew her, which was strange because she couldn't remember ever having seen him until a couple of days before, when she'd looked up at the cathedral walls near the doors and had seen what appeared to be a cat or a dog looking down at her. She'd almost turned around to raise the alarm when she'd realized it was a small gargoyle. She had laughed it off at the time, waving at it jauntily as if admonishing it for scaring her.

So she'd been surprised to find it inside the storeroom. Unless it was a different gargoyle. Maybe there were only a few different forms, and they were repeated throughout the building.

No, she was certain it was the same gargoyle because of the broken tongue, but even more, because she just felt it. The gargoyle cared for her, for reasons she couldn't understand.

You need to go out on a date, she told herself. *You're starting to go crazy.*

It wasn't as if she didn't have plenty of dating opportunities. Most of the men in the office had hit on her, married as well as unmarried: a bunch of ill-bred Italian-American men who had shown her that they didn't have the slightest clue how to behave ethically. They were all a bunch of crooks, and she'd rather be lonely than go out with any of them.

She'd gone to a couple of bars, and men had approached her, but it had seemed a little creepy, even after a few drinks. She'd never had a one-night stand, and she figured she was a little too old to be starting now.

Though if the alternative is talking to gargoyles, perhaps I should reconsider.

Father Gregory was watching her, as if expecting her to ask a question. "About the gargoyles..." she began. Her cellphone rang, and despite all the dampening tapestries and furnishings, the sound echoed loudly.

Mary pulled the phone out of her purse and looked at the number. It was the office. She continued to let it ring, and then turned it off.

"Would you do me a favor?" she asked the priest. "If my office calls here, tell them that cellphones don't work inside the cathedral. Because of all the stone and stuff?"

"You're asking a priest to lie?" Father Gregory looked shocked until she started to apologize, then he broke into a wry grin. "Of course, Mary. I understand a person trying to get away from work, even if I'm sort of in a job where that never happens. Do you want me to tell them you aren't here?"

"Don't do that," she said. "They'll think I'm lying. Just tell them that I can't be easily reached."

He nodded and sat back down in his desk. She turned to leave, and glanced back from the door to see that the Father was already picking up the budget papers again.

She made her way to the storeroom.

As she trudged up the stairs, she met another priest coming down. He was tall and thin, with a beaky nose, and in his black robes, he looked like a giant crow from Mary's perspective below him.

"Who are you? Are we letting just anyone wander our cathedral these days?" he asked.

"I'm Mary Patronis. I'm cleaning the gargoyles."

"Why on earth would you want to do that?" he demanded.

"Are you Father Michael?" Mary asked in as sweet a voice as she could manage. "Don't worry, you don't have to pay me. I'm volunteering."

He peered at her suspiciously. "Are you one of our parishioners, young lady?'

"Not yet," Mary found herself saying. She almost said yes. After all, Father Gregory had insisted that she was an honorary Catholic. *Please don't ask for specifics*, she thought.

"Did the Conservation Committee send you?" the priest demanded.

Mary didn't answer, letting it seem like it was true. She hadn't technically lied, and it kept the arrangement between her and Father Gregory secret.

"Ah," the priest intoned. "I should have known. Well, I don't suppose it does any harm. I suppose I should thank you." He held out his hand, and Mary wasn't sure if she was supposed to shake it or kiss it.

She shook it, and his hand lingered a little too long in hers.

"If you need anything," he said softly, "please come see me in my office." He reached out and brushed her cheek, his fingers coming near her mouth.

Mary had little doubt that he was coming on to her. *Hmmm*, she thought. *I must just attract these kinds of men.* She managed not to shudder as she passed by the priest, who made no effort to move aside. She brushed against him, making sure to turn to her side. Then she went on up the stairs, feeling the priest's eyes appraising her backside. She stopped at the small bathroom and filled the pail with soap and hot water, and rinsed out the brush in the sink. Cleaning seemed to also wash away the dirty memory of Father Michael's unwanted caress.

Mary hummed to herself. It a strange way, the physical labor felt good. Few would appreciate her effort, and yet it seemed worthy to her. These gargoyles would be gracing the cathedral long after she was dead and gone, and she would have had a hand in its beauty and grace.

She reached the door to the storeroom and stopped. It seemed to her that she'd heard voices on the other side. She threw open the door, and it was as if she'd walked into the middle of a conversation. Yet there was no one there.

The gargoyles were waiting for her. *Of course they are*, she thought ruefully. *Where are they going to go?*

The small gargoyle she had cleaned the week before appeared to be wide-awake and on the verge of speaking. His wide eyes stared at her with stony appraisal. His forehead was furrowed in thought.

"Hello, Mr. Gargoyle," she said. "Have you had pleasant dreams?"

Chapter 11

"There you are, Dominic!" Alastair the ghost exclaimed as he popped into view at the center of the room, followed a few moments later by Margerie. "We thought we'd lost you forever."

"Dashed to pieces on the sidewalk, we feared," Margerie added. The female ghost frowned and gave him a sideways look. "You're looking rather dapper."

"Best he's ever looked," Alastair said. "I see the traces of human care upon your brow, lucky gargoyle."

"I...uh..." Dominic didn't know how to respond. He thought perhaps he'd seen the last of his pestering ghosts, but they'd tracked him down.

Margerie walked/floated up to him. "You're looking very pleased with yourself," she mused. She bent down and passed her incorporeal hand across his brow as if she was petting him. Then she snatched the hand back, looking surprised. "Someone who cares has been touching you. Someone you care about as well. Don't tell me your lady friend has found you!"

"If it's any of your business," a gruff voice said from the other side of the room. Grotesque sounded annoyed. "You must be the ghosts that Dominic here has been talking about. I thought perhaps you were part of his delusion. Yet here you are...as real as the morning mist."

Margerie cried out in surprise and soared up to the ceiling and halfway through it, so that only her long skirt and high-heeled, long-laced shoes were showing. Then she floated back down, looking embarrassed at her reaction. "You might have introduced yourself, sir," she said.

"We thought only Dominic was conscious," Alastair explained. "Then again, we've never tried talking to any of the other gargoyles. I suspect they don't have much interesting to say."

"There are more of us," Pretty said from the corner.

This time is was Alastair who was surprised, and he whirled around in a near panic. Though weightless, he had the mannerisms of an overweight, overdressed middle-aged man with a touch of gout in one leg. He carried a cane, and it sometimes seemed to Dominic that he could hear the clicking of the brass tip upon the stones of the cathedral.

"I suppose we've had no reason to talk to people who aren't really there," Pretty said, sounding amused.

"Delighted to meet you, gentle sirs," Alastair said, regaining his composure and bowing. "My name is Alastair Hamilton, and the young lady is named Margerie Marcotte."

"Grotesque," the bigger gargoyle answered.

"Indeed she is," Alastair said. "Though I would never be so blunt."

"No," Grotesque rumbled. "That is what I am called."

"And I'm Pretty," the smaller gargoyle said.

"Indeed…and exaggerated in one instance and understated in the other, I'm sure," Alastair said.

Grotesque and Pretty both seemed to be trying to work out if they'd been insulted or complimented. Since the comment could be interpreted either way, they both decided to ignore it.

Dominic wasn't sure he wanted his new and his old acquaintances being friends. Bad enough that he was stuck with a couple of strange gargoyles; the idea of having the ghosts nattering in his oversized ears at the same time was alarming.

"Someone's coming!" Margerie exclaimed, and both ghosts blinked out of view.

The door to the storeroom opened. Mary Patronis stood at the entrance, staring at Dominic. Then she smiled and walked over to him, putting her soft palms on his head.

"Hello, Mr. Gargoyle. Have you had pleasant dreams?"

In his mind's eye, Dominic closed his eyes and groaned at her touch. But of course, no sound emerged, and as ever, his eyes bulged in mute torment. He felt like he was almost vibrating, he wanted to speak so badly. He wanted to greet her, to talk to her, to touch her, to lick her hand with his broken tongue.

She set down the pail of hot water and dipped the stiff brush into it. Then she dripped the soapy water down over Dominic's head until every part of him was wet. She leaned back on her heels and nodded with satisfaction.

"We'll just let that soak in, Mr. Gargoyle," she said. "So...what do you want to talk about?"

Dominic so wanted to answer that question that it felt like it was breaking him in half. A large chunk of the guano on his back fell to the floor with a splat. Mary jumped slightly and frowned. Then she dipped the brush in the water again and held it over his head, dripping the water down.

"This is good, honest labor," she said. "Not like my other job. I'm ashamed of that job, though it pays the bills..." She hesitated. "I'm sure you don't want to hear about that."

Yes, tell me! Please tell me! Dominic wanted to scream, and something of that urging must have reached her.

"I didn't know what I was getting into when I got that job," she said. "I thought they were just a real estate company. High end, you know, but that's why they were paying so much. I thought...I feared they were only paying me for my looks, because it would please the rich people who came into the office. But they really didn't care about that. Turns out, most of the time, the agents go to the rich people, not the other way around."

She paused, lifted the brush, and started brushing Dominic's back, taking off the small chunks that the large slough of muck had left.

"So then I began to believe they really did appreciate my secretarial skills, and I was pleased."

She stopped again, deep in thought. The brush bristles lay against Dominic's neck, and it seemed to him that he could feel them pushing into the stone, as if the darkness of her thoughts was adding weight to them.

"It didn't take me long to realize they didn't care about my accounting skills either. Only one thing mattered to them. My silence."

Mary roused herself and started brushing again, and continued until another big chunk came off of Dominic's belly. Now only the guano on his feet remained, and the gargoyle suddenly realized with alarm that when Mary was done, she would have no reason to touch him, to talk to him again. That she would move on to the other gargoyles, the ones who couldn't really feel or appreciate her touch.

Grotesque and Pretty had fallen silent. It was becoming clear to him that they, along with the ghosts, only manifested when he was alone. *Are they even real?* He wondered. *Are they simply a product of my loneliness?*

No, he decided. Might as well question his own existence, which was equally impossible.

"It is so easy to stay silent," Mary said. "They give me regular raises. They trust me more and more. And the more they pay, the more they trust me, the more I am ashamed."

She leaned back again and looked up toward the ceiling, as if embarrassed to meet Dominic's eyes. "I started going with some of the agents on their rounds. At first, I thought it must be a mistake. Surely they meant to fix the problems. Then I realized that it was all planned. The contracts, the fines, the penalties, all were meant to squeeze the maximum profit from the most vulnerable of people. I thought they were a high-end real estate company, and they are...for the select few. But for the rest, they are slumlords. Worse than slumlords, for slumlords at least provide housing. My employers take the money and almost never deliver."

She picked up the brush and started brushing hard against parts of Dominic that had already been cleaned, but that wasn't the point. She was brushing to forget, to erase the thoughts from her mind. But it wasn't working.

"I came to this city to be an actress. I wasn't good enough. Or perhaps I wasn't hungry enough. But some of those workshop lessons must have sunk in, because even when I witnessed the greatest of injustices, I kept my cheery smile. And I got another raise."

She closed her eyes, and tears were squeezed out to drip down her cheeks.

"I can't do it anymore," she whispered.

Dominic was helpless. *Remove this curse,* he cried out in his mind. *Not for my sake, but for hers!*

She sighed and looked at her watch. "Oh, dear. Not making much progress, am I? I think I'll let you soak for a bit, Mr. Gargoyle, while I get started on another." She stood and looked around the room. Somehow it wasn't a surprise to him when, out of all the many gargoyles left to clean, she chose Grotesque. Dominic could almost sense the other gargoyle's pleasure, though it was muted by Mary's presence.

Dominic watched as she started cleaning the other gargoyle. Water was still dripping off his head, and the rivulets felt like the tears he was feeling inside.

Grant me life, he prayed. *So that I might help her.*

But the cathedral simply loomed around him, as huge and heavy and silent as ever. He was merely stone, and nothing in this world or the next cared what he thought.

He could almost feel the words coming to his mouth, as if they would actually be uttered. But at that moment, the door opened, and Jon Williams entered.

Chapter 12

Jon couldn't stop thinking about the gargoyles. They were leftovers from another time, and yet it was as if he understood them and what they represented, as if they appealed to a more primitive, instinctive part of his nature, the part of him that had been drawn to art only to find that he was hopeless at creating his own.

But he could appreciate art, and he'd made a slight detour into art history, which satisfied both his intellect and his soul. The gargoyles were everything that had drawn him to the field. They spoke to him. He snorted. *No, really, one if the gargoyles* spoke *to me!*

"Where's your head at?" his advisor, Tom Huffington, asked. As Jon came back to the present, he realized that the question had been asked more than once. They were sitting in Dr. Huffington's cluttered office. The floor and desk were covered with books, and Jon was fighting an unending battle to keep one of the chairs clear — a battle he was losing. He hated to think what would greet his mentor's next graduate assistant.

"Sorry," he said. "I've been thinking about the gargoyles." He'd told Huffington about his discovery of the storeroom, but the professor had seemed unimpressed. "How come no one has studied them?"

"What's to study?" Professor Huffington was only a decade older than Jon, but he seemed like a real adult. In Jon's mind, he always thought of his mentor as Doctor or Professor, even if he addressed him as Tom. The man always wore a rumpled corduroy suit and bright bowtie, and his hair was long on top so that it flopped over his forehead in a way that made him constantly toss his head back. The habit had driven Jon to distraction at first, but now it just seemed part of him. "The gargoyles were carved by unknown craftsmen. No one knows their names, and if they did, no one would know who carved what."

"Have they been searched for attribution, Tom? Or has everyone simply assumed there is nothing there?"

"Well, you're certainly welcome to look...on your own time. Of which you have none. You've got three weeks to finish your dissertation before you catch that plane to Barcelona. I'm jealous, by the way."

Yeah, you always say that, Jon thought. *But you love your little tenured office.*

"You really should look at them," he insisted. "The pictures don't do them justice. You say craftsmen carved them; I say master artisans."

Tom shrugged. "You say tomato, I say potato. Like I said, you can check the gargoyles on your own time, or during your work shifts."

Jon had only one week left to work, and Harding had implied that he'd have light duties. "Yeah, I think I might do that. I think they are the embodiment of my thesis."

The professor looked up at him, as if interested in the conversation for the first time. "You mean, how the gargoyles began as superstitious manifestations and ended up as utilitarian structures."

"They were always at least partly utilitarian," Jon said. "But yeah, it seems to me that if my thesis is that the building of cathedrals overlapped from the Dark Ages to the Age of Enlightenment, then the gargoyles are perfect representations of that divide."

"Interesting..." Huffington intoned. Then he shook his head. "Listen, Jon. You're already almost done with your dissertation. From what I've read so far, I'd say you're a shoo-in. Probably best not to upset the apple cart now."

"I hope you're right," Jon said. He'd never been quite sure about his advisor's pull with the rest of the faculty. They seemed to ignore the bow-tied man during functions, but it was possible that Dr. Huffington was ignoring *them*. "Never hurts to have one more example."

"Then I think our business is done," Huffington said, rising and extending his hand. Jon was startled, because his professor had never done that before. "It's going to get crazier and crazier for you over the next few weeks, so I just wanted to tell you now how much I've enjoyed having you as my assistant. I don't usually...make friends."

Jon was unexpectedly moved. Huffington had always been kind of a cold fish, though he tried.

"Thank you, Tom. I've been honored."

They stood there awkwardly for few moments after the handshake. Then Jon turned abruptly and headed for the door without looking back. "See you next week," he said over his shoulder as he left.

But instead of going home, he found himself walking toward the cathedral. The university was ostensibly a Catholic institution, though it was run in a mostly secular way. The cathedral could be seen from almost anywhere on campus.

He was supposed to go home and sweat over his thesis. He wasn't due at work for another few days, and all his teaching classes were over. Everyone would be expecting him to have the traditional nervous breakdown over the pressure.

Truth was, he'd finished the paper months ago, but had decided it would not do to make it look too easy. So he'd pretended to keep working on it, giving Professor Huffington pieces at a time, while he was home reading mysteries.

Now he regretted not submitting the dissertation earlier. He was going to have to fly home from Spain to defend it, with money he didn't have. He laughed out loud, getting some strange looks from undergraduates on the path. He was already so far in debt from his undergraduate days that he'd be paying for the rest of his life. The only good thing about being a poor art major graduate student was that he couldn't get any poorer.

He let himself in the side door, deciding he really didn't want to run into any of his coworkers. They'd undoubtedly have something they "needed" his help with. Never go into work on your day off, his father had once told him.

In his eagerness to see the gargoyles again, Jon took two stairs at a time up the spiral staircase. He marched down the hallway and threw open the door to the storeroom, expecting to have the rest of the afternoon to himself to study the gargoyles.

Instead, there was a young woman leaning over one of the larger gargoyles, scrubbing away at the creature's extended tongue with a stiff brush. She looked over her shoulder with a smile, as if expecting someone else. The smile dropped as she realized he wasn't who she thought he was.

But it was too late. In that flash of smile, Jon was lost.

Chapter 13

Jon stood at the doorway of the storeroom, speechless.

The woman was blonde and blue-eyed, with delicate features. A long, thin nose was the only thing that disturbed the perfection of her face, and yet, that nose added an exotic cast to her beauty. She was small, but had a nice figure. She didn't wear makeup, but then, she didn't need to. Jon felt an overwhelming desire to get to know her.

Don't blow this, he thought to himself, and immediately felt the old familiar panic.

The woman turned and nodded to him, nervously, and began taking off her gloves, as if to shake his hands. "I'm Mary," she said.

Jon pre-empted her by waving at her shyly. "Jon. Sorry, I didn't know anyone was in here."

"Understandable," she said. "From the amount of dust, I doubt more than two or three people have been in here in years. Me and Father Gregory and some of the workmen who brought in the gargoyles, I suppose."

"I...I've been working here for over a year, and I didn't even know this room existed until a couple of days ago," Jon admitted.

"You brought some of the gargoyles here?"

Jon looked around for the small gargoyle, and almost didn't recognize it because it was so shiny and new-looking. Again, the sense that the gargoyle was watching, was appraising him, was overwhelming. This time, the gargoyle seemed to be disapproving.

Jealous? Jon wondered, and then wondered why he'd thought such a silly thing.

"Just this little fella," he said. He almost put his hand down on the gargoyle's head, then changed his mind at the last moment.

Mary seemed to notice his hesitation. "He's really something, isn't he?" she said, staring into Jon's eyes.

"Almost like he's alive," Jon agreed.

Mary looked startled, and then flustered. She dipped the brush into the water pail and turned back to the gargoyle she'd been working on.

Jon watched her work, feeling awkward and yet not wanting to leave. There was something about her, as if she was thinking the same thing about these gargoyles as he was. But even more...as if she thought about the cathedral and about art and about life the same as he did. Why he thought that, he didn't know. But it was as if they were connected somehow.

"Sometimes it's as if they are talking to me," Mary said, her face turned away. She looked over her shoulder at Jon as if testing his reaction to her statement.

"I know what you mean," he said.

"Do you?" She stood up and dropped the brush into the bucket. She put her hands on her hips and stared at him frankly. He wanted to step toward her, just to be closer to her, but somehow resisted.

I'm leaving town in a few more weeks, he thought. *I have no time to get to know anyone.*

Yet why did he have the feeling that she was someone whom he was destined to know? Not only know, but *know*...intimately. He blushed and looked away. But just as he turned his eyes away, he saw a speculative look come into her eyes.

"You need some more hot water?" he asked.

"That would be great," she said.

Jon grabbed the pail and headed out the door. He practically ran to the bathroom in a panic. As he ran the water, waiting for it to get hot, he tried to gather himself. He'd always been shy around girls, but never like this. He'd been able to hang back in the past, let the girls come to him. They liked his shyness, so it worked.

But he sensed that with this woman, it wouldn't work. She was suspicious of him, of all men. How he could know this, he didn't know. But it was as if he could read her mind, feel her emotions. She'd been hurt recently. An ex-husband or boyfriend had hurt her, and she wasn't inclined to get to know another man anytime soon.

Good, he thought. *Just as well.*

Still, as he carried the pail back, his felt his heart speeding up, and he wracked his brain for something clever to say. Instead, the second he entered the room, he blurted out, "Would you like to go out for coffee sometime? To talk about the gargoyles?"

Mary didn't look disgusted by his question, but she didn't look eager either. "Why are you here, exactly?" she asked.

"Oh, right. Sorry. I'm a graduate student. The college got me a job with the maintenance crew to help pay for school. I'm studying the cathedral's architecture."

"Including the gargoyles?" Mary asked, sounding interested for the first time.

"Yeah," Jon said. "Like I said, I didn't even know this room existed. So this is a whole new area for me to explore. Though…well, I'm leaving in a few weeks for postgraduate studies in Europe."

Did a little bit of disappointment flicker over her face, or did he imagine it? She hadn't answered his question about a date. He bent down and lifted the brush out of the steaming water, and as he did so, he put his other hand on the top of the gargoyle for balance. They touched hands, and both of them froze.

Jon wanted to reach out and take both her hands, and if she was reading his mind, she shoved them into the pockets of her smock.

"Look, I'm busy," she said. "I have to get this done."

"Oh, sure," he heard himself saying. "I'll get out of your hair."

When she didn't answer right away, Jon fled.

As he spun down the stairs, he cursed himself. He'd done the opposite of what he wanted to do. What he'd envisioned in his mind was sitting and having a nice chat, talking about gargoyles and the cathedral and oh, by the way, are you single?

But of course, he'd done the opposite, as usual. *This is why you can't have nice things*, he thought. *Or nice women.*

He stopped, took a deep breath, and tried to control his panic. Should he go back? But how would he explain his flight?

Reluctantly, he continued down the stairs and out of the cathedral, and walked back to his room alone.

Chapter 14

Mary hadn't really expected the young man to run away, despite what she'd said. She had turned to keep cleaning the gargoyle, and by the time she'd turned back with an apology on her lips, he was gone.

Now she stood in the center of the room, trying to shake the feeling that she was being watched. The two gargoyles she had already cleaned, the small one by the door and the big one across from it, had seemed to come alive in her hands. It all would have seemed a pathetic illusion brought on by her fear and loneliness but for that guy, Jon, apparently feeling the same thing.

She turned her back on the two gargoyles and selected one near the center of the room that was worn and dirty and emanated not the slightest sense of life. She touched it gingerly, and relief flooded through her when she felt nothing. She carried the pail of water over to it and started scraping away.

Mary took a deep breath and put her back into it. It was strange to be feeling such strong emotions. Ever since Peter had died, she'd been feeling hollow. Oh, there was the pervading sense of dread that came from the realization of what bad people she was working for, and at the same time, paradoxically, the fear of losing her job, but that was a low-grade feeling that was always there.

These new emotions were strong and pure. She was interested in something other than survival for the first time in a long time. It was somehow giving her the courage to think that perhaps, just perhaps, she could quit her job, get away, and start all over again.

Maybe I really am turning Catholic, she mused. *I'm starting to believe in redemption and the cleansing away of my sins.*

But it was the jolt of attraction that she'd felt for Jon Williams that surprised her the most. Despite her loneliness, she hadn't *really* considered going out on a date with any man since Peter had died.

I didn't give him an answer, she suddenly realized. *He asked me out, and I evaded the question.*

Jon seemed like a nice guy. Even more importantly, he hadn't automatically assumed that she was crazy when she'd talked about the gargoyle's being alive.

Scared off another one, she thought.

He'd been good looking, with short brown hair, a long beard, and dark brown eyes. He was wearing a t-shirt and cargo shorts. His lanky body had some interesting muscles in the shoulders and arms, and he had nicely formed legs.

"Maybe that's what I need," she said to the smaller gargoyle, whom she could feel staring at her back. "A nice college-type guy. Someone who will appreciate me for the woman I am."

She dipped the brush into the water.

Talking to gargoyles. Just how lonely am I?

Mary stood up and looked at the big gargoyle, who, though crouched over, was nearly as tall as she was. It was difficult to reach the back of the creature with the brush. Her arms weren't long enough. She tentatively tried to turn the sculpture around. With great effort, she managed to tip it slightly and roll it onto its edge. As she was doing so, she felt resistance—and not just because of the weight of the creature. It was almost as if the gargoyle itself was protesting.

"Don't want to be staring at the wall?" she said out loud, then wondered why the thought had occurred to her. *It's stone. It doesn't care.*

Yet, when she was done with the cleaning, she put the gargoyle back in the same position it had been in before, though it required a great effort on her part.

She felt like she was among friends. *Be friendly,* she thought. *Treat them nice.*

"Okay, I'm officially losing it," she muttered. "Next guy who asks me out, I'm going. I don't care who he is. Except Mario...or Antonio...or Sergio. Or...well, *any* of those Italian bastards at her office."

That pretty much eliminates all possible candidates for dating, she thought ruefully. *Who else do I know?*

Once again, Jon's face came to her. She tried to remember his features exactly, but they were already blurring. She'd probably lost her chance with him.

She looked around for the next gargoyle to clean, and while she was considering, drifted over to the first small gargoyle she'd worked on and laid her hand on its head companionably. It seemed crazy, but it was as if she could read its thoughts. The little thing was madly in love with her.

Mary shook her head, amazed at her delusion and the form it took. *I'm so desperate for a friend that I've chosen a lump of carved rock. An ugly lump at that.*

"Poor thing," she said. "Losing your tongue like that."

I can still speak.

She cried out, lifting her hand off the gargoyle as if it was a hot coal. She backed away toward the door and stared at the sculpture. The bigger gargoyle was looking right at her, and it seemed to her that it was laughing.

She approached the small gargoyle and tentatively reached out with a single finger and touched its head again.

I won't hurt you.

Mary lifted the finger off its head. She went to where she'd laid her coat down and, without looking at anything else, put it on. She grabbed the bucket and brush and left the storeroom, closing the door firmly behind her.

"Leaving early?"

Mary started at the voice. She'd been standing in the middle of the hallway for she didn't know how long. The pail of water was heavy, and she felt the grooves of the handle cutting into her palm. She set the pail down and turned.

Father Gregory looked concerned. She tried to put on a brave smile.

"I was just getting some fresh hot water," she said.

"In your coat?"

She blushed, and then found herself admitting the truth. "I was a little spooked. Do you ever find yourself thinking that inanimate objects are alive?"

The priest looked at her curiously, but not as if he thought she was crazy. "It's human nature to anthropomorphize things," he said. "But as it happens, I know exactly what you mean. I've often felt that this cathedral was talking to me, as if it was haunted. Which I suppose it must be. As a believer, I shouldn't be surprised if it is imbued by the Holy Spirit, should I?"

Mary frowned. She wasn't a believer, so his explanation wasn't very comforting. As though the priest could read her mind, he continued.

"Even if I wasn't a believer in God and the Holy Spirit, I still think finding consciousness in that which is solid is not so unusual. It's just ourselves reflecting our own thoughts back to us."

Is that all it is? she wondered. But even as she grasped at that hope, she didn't really believe it.

"I was just coming to check on you," Father Gregory said. "Making much progress?"

"It's harder work than I thought," she said. "It's going to take a long time to clean them all."

"Well, remember, don't feel as if you have to do it," he said. As he spoke, he started walking toward the storeroom, and without thinking, Mary followed. "I mean, I'm appreciative of all the work, but it really isn't your job."

"No, I'm happy to do it," she said quickly. Spooked or not, she found she really wanted to continue.

"How is your other problem?" Father Gregory asked.

Mary regretted she'd said anything to the priest. The cathedral was her escape, but she'd brought her real-world problems within its walls.

"The same," she said. "I think…I know you're right, Father. I should go to the authorities. But…I need the money."

"Is that the only reason?" he asked.

He'd jumped right past her excuse to the truth beneath. She was frightened. These men were dangerous; she'd understood that from the beginning. All along, there had been employees showing up in the office with mysterious injuries; worse, some employees didn't show back up at work at all, and no one was willing to explain what had happened. Something bad, she was pretty sure.

They reached the storeroom. As they stood at the threshold, Mary hesitated. What would she see? What would she hear?

Father Gregory opened the door casually and stepped in. After a moment, she followed.

Nope, just rocks. Dumb rocks. Rocks can't speak; rocks don't think.

She felt relief wash over her, but at the same time, underneath it all, she realized she was also vaguely disappointed.

"Since we…you…started this little project, I've been doing some research," Father Gregory said, staring at the large, newly cleaned gargoyle. "This cathedral was built over many years, so the smaller gargoyles lower down were placed first. There are some interesting stories about them. Just in the years it took to complete this building, civilization seemed to pass from superstition to the Enlightenment. The early stories are more interesting, though."

He obviously wanted her to ask, so she prompted him, "What kind of stories?"

"Well, it's funny you should ask about gargoyles being alive, because the legend is that the early ones were humans cursed into the shape of gargoyles for their past sins." Father Gregory looked around the room until he saw the first small gargoyle that she'd cleaned. "So this little fellow was once a man."

He reached out and patted the gargoyle on the head, and Mary winced. She waited for a reaction, but the priest simply gave her a crooked smile as if to ask, "How preposterous is that?"

Instead of being reassured, though, she felt herself becoming excited by the idea. "Can I read the books those stories are in?" she asked. "I mean, it might be fun to know the history behind these creatures."

The priest frowned. "I...I probably shouldn't, but really, I can't see why not. You can't take them out of the cathedral, though."

"I promise," she said. "Can we go get them right now?"

"Our archives are in the lower chambers," he said. "I'll lead the way." He left the room without looking back.

Mary hesitated at the door and looked back at the gargoyle.

I am your friend, it seemed to be saying.

She shuddered and followed Father Gregory out the door.

Chapter 15

I am your friend! Dominic cried out.

Mary paused at the doorway. Then she was gone.

Dominic felt the old rage returning, feeling so furious he couldn't summon a word or a thought. He felt as if his soul had just been buried under stone, cast into darkness.

He could forget, sometimes, what had brought him to this state: the anger, the jealousy, the violent reaction to anyone who tried to take what was his—or more dangerously, *who* was his.

He'd felt the young man's yearning for Mary—and worse, he'd felt her respond. There had been a brief flash of interest between the two humans. It was only a beginning, but Dominic knew where such beginnings led. He'd seen it before and had been helpless to stop it. He had watched it play out until the woman he loved walked out of his life and into the arms of another man.

Mary's voice in the hallway, talking to the priest, receded into the distance. Dominic struggled to dismiss his jealousy, the same green-eyed fiend that had caused this curse in the first place.

For once, his gargoyle companions were silent. Even Grotesque was too stunned to say anything. Dominic couldn't see Pretty's face, but felt the sense of wonder emanating from the corner. Suddenly, he realized why they were amazed, and for the moment, his jealousy receded as he too marveled at the miracle.

Mary heard me! There was no doubt. She'd responded just as if he'd spoken aloud. Whatever magic had awoken him and attuned him to her emotions had somehow also reached her. She'd been frightened off for now, but for the first time, Dominic was certain she would return.

In those few seconds of touching, he'd felt her whirl of emotions, not only about what was happening in the moment, but also about what was happening in her life outside the cathedral.

She's in danger, he realized as he mulled over what he'd absorbed. *She senses the menace, but also diminishes it.* Dominic, perhaps because he came from a more brutal time, recognized the threat instantly and understood that it needed to be dealt with, either confronted or escaped. Mary wanted to leave the place of danger, but he could tell that she hadn't yet made the decision to do that.

"How is it possible?" Pretty said, finally. "Such a thing has never happened."

"Because you know everything?" Grotesque scoffed.

"I know that if such a thing had ever happened before, the priests would have noticed; it would have been written about, it would be part of the lore. This has never happened, Grotesque, so keep your ignorance to yourself."

Grotesque snorted, but didn't say anything more. Pretty continued, speaking to Dominic. "When you told us that you had once been human, I thought you were making it up. But now I can see no other explanation. Whatever curse turned you into one of our kind is somehow weakening because of this woman. I believe you may escape our eternal fate, Dominic. You can become mortal once again."

"'Until you love someone more than you love yourself, you shall be damned to eternal silence,'" Dominic intoned.

"Was that the curse?" Pretty asked.

Dominic didn't answer.

"Do you want to tell us what it means?" Pretty persisted.

"No," Dominic said.

Despite himself, the memories came flooding back, memories he'd succeeded in burying behind his stone surface for two centuries.

It had been so unexpected when Katherine had left him. One moment he was happy, thinking that he was the luckiest of men to have found a woman who loved him as much as he loved her. The next moment he realized he'd been deluded, a simple cuckold. Stray

73

comments and laughter over the previous days suddenly came back to him, things people had said that had been puzzling at the time, and somehow disturbing, but that he'd been able to dismiss.

Dominic had felt paralyzed by the notion that everyone had known but him, that they'd been snickering behind his back. He'd thought he had gained her heart, but she had duped him, and now his trust seemed foolish.

But the true pain came from the loss of Katherine's love. He felt empty, as if the spirit that had once filled him with peace vanished in an instant. He was alone again, more alone than before he'd met her. It wasn't jealousy, not really; jealousy would imply that there was a competition, that he had a chance of regaining her love. No, it was pure anguish at the thought the he would never again have her.

Perhaps if he'd had a suspicion, any inkling at all, it wouldn't have hurt so much. But it had been so unexpected: walking into the sitting room with a smile on his face, a story he'd wanted to tell—and which he could never remember afterward—and seeing them clinched together, fully pressed together from lips to…to…

He blanked out on that vision sometimes. It was forever burned into his memory, but at the same time, it was blurry, as if he couldn't fully face the magnitude of it. There was no explaining it away. There was no misapprehension about what he'd seen, and all three parties knew it.

Without a word, she had moved out that night, and he'd never seen her again…until that last fateful day.

He shut down the memory, closed it off inside the stone, and as he did so, he felt himself losing consciousness, returning to his inactive state.

"Dominic!" he heard Grotesque grunt, and he struggled to remember why he was there and why he was awake, why the painful memories of his condition were returning. He stirred himself, acknowledging the pain but at the same time refusing to relive the details.

He'd had decades to reflect on his guilt, and yet he'd thought about the actual event not at all. He refused to. There was no sense obsessing over his sin or what it all meant. His punishment was just. He regretted his actions and was willing to atone for them. He was remorseful.

Or was he? For the first time since he'd been frozen into this shape, he wondered. Thinking about someone else's troubles made him wonder if he was truly repentant or merely regretting his punishment.

It didn't matter. Mary needed his help, and he was helpless to do anything.

Reluctantly, to his own amazement, Dominic began to consider whether his connection to Jon Williams was part of the answer. His link to the man had seemed random, as much an inconvenience as a miracle. It had confused him, but he'd decided that their blood bond was meaningless.

Until now. Now he saw that these events were fated. Jon Williams could move freely, while Dominic could not. Jon could be reached and told of the danger, and could do something about it.

Dominic would have to overcome his jealous rage for Mary's sake. He didn't have to like it, or like the man, but if Jon could save Mary, then he'd have to find a way to accept it.

"You must scare that young man away, Dominic," Alastair said, popping into the middle of the room. "You're going to lose her."

Grotesque laughed. "He can't lose what he never had."

"Oh?" Alastair said. "Is that how you feel, Dominic?"

"Be quiet, you," Margerie said, appearing alongside the other ghost. "Leave Dominic alone. You know how it hurts him."

"You know what happened?" Pretty asked. "Dominic here has been rather reticent about telling us."

"Alastair," Margerie warned, but the blustery ghost ignored her.

"His wife left him for another man. Dominic shot them dead. I should hate him for that, for…well, that's why I'm a ghost. But I believe Dominic has been punished quite enough."

The silence in the room was that of the cathedral as a human might have felt it, empty and echoing. It was as if every ghost, every gargoyle had heard Alastair's words and was waiting for Dominic's response.

"She's in danger," Dominic said. "She is not mine; she was never mine. I must help her."

"Well, then," Pretty said. "We'll have to find a way to help you."

Chapter 16

"I'll need to stop by my office and get the keys," Father Gregory said. "It can be rather alarming down there, I warn you."

"Alarming?" Mary repeated.

"Well, you'll have to see it for yourself, but it isn't for the faint of heart."

"I'm sure I'll be fine," Mary said.

The keys turned out to be a set of old-fashioned skeleton keys strung on a pitted old iron circle. A single piece of flat plastic also hung from the keychain, looking completely out of place.

The staircase to Father Gregory's office was made of concrete, wide and flat. But as soon as they left those comfy surroundings and went down one more level, the stairs became narrower and were made of stone. There were furrows worn into their surface, and Father Gregory warned Mary that it was easy to be tipped off balance. She kept one hand on the wall, and realized, as they descended, that other people had been doing the same thing for decades, for there was a groove in the wall as well. The stairs wound downward, getting narrower and steeper as they went.

There was a string of bare electric bulbs in the low ceiling, with the wires showing. It felt as if they were descending into a large well, for the air become cool and humid. There were small tunnels off to the sides every level or so, which even Mary would have had to crouch to fit into.

"When they built the lower levels of the cathedral, people were smaller," Gregory explained.

They had descended about three levels before the first cave appeared. It was off to one side, and all that separated the stairs from the drop-off was an old, rickety wooden barrier. The huge chamber was filled with broken stalactites and stalagmites littering the floor.

"I've been told that this was once quite beautiful, but some school kids on a fieldtrip went a little wild and destroyed it all," the priest explained. "My predecessors weren't the stewards they should have been."

The next cave-like opening was on the other side, one level down. There was a small flight of stairs down into the rounded chamber, and the walls were speckled with white, as if the rampaging school kids had scribbled on the stone with chalk. Then Mary's eyes adjusted and focused on the white objects, and she realized with a start what they were.

What she noticed first was the femurs, stacked like cords of wood along one wall. The skulls were in the back, which was why she hadn't seen them. They stared at her, most of them missing their lower jaws, yet seeming to scream. She gasped, and Father Gregory nodded his head. "They stopped using these catacombs in the last century, but you see before you two hundred years of Catholic remains. So if you ever wondered if the cathedral is haunted, here's your answer. I never fail to feel the weight of these lives when I'm down here."

"How far does this go down?" she asked.

"To the foundations," he said. "Which is no answer, is it? Let's see…about two more levels of stairs. There are some tunnels that go deeper, but I'm too chicken to check them out. There are stories…"

They stood staring at the bones a little longer, and Mary became slightly ashamed by her fright. They were just the remains of people, people like her. It was what happened to everyone. Nothing to be scared of.

There was a tunnel on the opposite side of the crypt, which had been widened and which appeared to have better, more modern lighting. "The archives are this way," Father Gregory said, starting off in that direction.

"Could we go all the way down first?" Mary heard herself asking, and was surprised at her own request. She'd always been attracted to cave hopping when she was a kid back in the High Desert of Oregon. She'd explored lava caves that went on for miles, some branches of which she was pretty sure no one else had been down before her. This brought back those pleasant memories of exploring with the neighbor kids before sex and popularity contests had interfered with their fun.

"I suppose," Father Gregory said. "We might get a little dirty. No one takes care of the lower chambers, and we've let the pumps that drain the water become inactive. In fact, that's the first item on the repairs budget. The water is going to reach the archives in another couple of decades."

They started down. Within a few steps, a huge wooden door, strapped with iron bonds, confronted them. For the first time, Father Gregory used one of the ancient keys on the circlet. The door opened with a creak that made Mary laugh nervously. It was as if they were entering a dungeon, the Father in his black robes leading the sinner to the doom of the torture chamber. The vapor that swept toward them from the other side of the door flattened Mary's hair to her skull. The water smelled of stone and earth.

"Watch out, the steps are slick," Father Gregory warned.

A thin film of slimy moisture covered the rock walls, and as Mary ran her hands along them, water began trickling down her sleeves. Father Gregory was obviously reluctant to go forward, but must have caught some of her eagerness, because he continued downward. "It is rather…medieval, I suppose you'd call it," he said, as they rounded a last curve of the stairs and reached the largest chamber yet. A single light at the end of the stairs, where they entered the water, was all that illuminated the huge space.

Mary let her eyes adjust and eventually saw that water filled the bottom of the chamber, black and seemingly as deep as the chasms of hell, though it was possible it was only a few feet deep. Out of the water jutted natural rock abutments, and on the flattened tops of these geological features, the cathedral builders had placed the structure's foundations.

"I've often wondered where the steps lead," Father Gregory said. "But I can't help but imagine tentacle monsters below that surface, guarding the gates to the underworld. Silly, I know. I read too much sci-fi and horror when I was a kid, I suppose. H.P. Lovecraft and the like."

Mary had never heard the name, but she still sensed what the priest meant. This place harkened back to a time before time, primeval, existing long before the foundations of the cathedral had been laid and never banished by all the religion practiced above it.

"Come," Father Gregory said, pointing upward. "We really shouldn't let too much of this moisture seep upward."

They climbed rapidly, as if ghosts were chasing them. Mary couldn't help but look nervously over her shoulder once or twice, and Father Gregory also took a couple of edgy glances backward.

When he slammed the door behind them, they both took a deep breath. He locked the door was a satisfying clank.

"Come," Father Gregory said, relief evident in his voice. "This way."

Within a few paces, they were in a modern tunnel. The walls had obviously been widened and reinforced in the near past, and instead of bare wires and bulbs, there were lights inset into the ceiling. They were confronted by another door, but this one was a modern door that had no keyhole. Father Gregory grabbed the plastic card and inserted it into the slot in the door. It opened with a hiss, as if there was air on the other side. Instead, within a few feet, there was another, identical door.

"An airlock?" Mary marveled.

"The air pressure on the other side keeps the moisture out," the priest said, closing the door behind them before approaching the other door and inserting the key card again. The second door opened with an even louder hiss, and suddenly the humidity disappeared. *It feels as dry as the High Desert on a summer day*, Mary thought.

And then they went back in time again, from the twenty-first century back hundreds of years. The walls of the archives were rough stone, and the lighting was bare bulbs, though there were more of them. The room was filled from top to bottom with books and manuscripts. One long table was covered with single pages weighed down with all manner of paperweights, ancient and modern, and ran along the nearest wall to the door.

"The airlock cost a decade of our maintenance budget," the priest said. "But it was decided that these manuscript were too precious to waste and too fragile to move." He kept moving into the room and turned to one side, and only then did Mary see the small opening to a second room.

This room was even more modernized. It had rock walls, but the furniture and equipment was up to date. There was a large computer monitor on one table, and Father Gregory went to the computer and turned it on.

"We have about twenty percent of the material scanned and digitalized so far," he said. "Really, I should be asking you if you want to do this instead of cleaning the gargoyles. It's probably more important."

"Beauty is important too," Mary said.

The priest looked at her and gave her a small smile. "I wouldn't have agreed with you a few months ago, but you've convinced me. Anyway, you wanted to see the archives, and here they are."

"Who's allowed down here?" she asked. She saw a smaller room carved into one side, and glimpsed a cot and table inside.

"Some of the staff and graduate students at the college, and occasionally a Jesuit from somewhere else, will drop by and spend some time down here. But to tell you the truth, it's empty probably ninety percent of the time."

"Would you...would you give me a key?" Mary asked. She wasn't even sure why she wanted one. She wasn't a scholar; she knew almost nothing about the Catholic faith that she hadn't read in stories or seen in movies. But this room felt comfortable, familiar. As if she was meant to be here.

Father Gregory shook his head. "I'm sorry. It's not allowed. Credentialed scholars only, and even they have to go through a vetting process. Father Michael is very...selective. It's all fascinating, I know, but not really for just the curious."

Mary didn't argue, but a plan began form in her mind. She'd been in Father Gregory's office several times now without anyone else being around. The keys were in the top—unlocked—drawer.

She didn't know how or why, but she was coming back.

Chapter 17

Mary was still shaking when she reached the storeroom. She closed the door gratefully behind her. She turned to the gargoyles, who, despite their fearsome appearance, felt like old friends.

"Hello, boys," she said, then laughed shakily. "Oh…if there are any ladies among you, sorry."

Then the strength seemed to go out of her legs, and she sat down in the middle of the room and put her head in her hands. Only now was she ready to start thinking about the ramifications of that morning.

She'd gone into work on her day off. Always a mistake, but she'd forgotten some paperwork and hoped she could just jet in and grab it and then scoot back out again. She'd been leaning over her desk drawer in her tiny cubicle when she'd heard the deep voice behind her.

"You're Mary Patronis, right?"

She turned reluctantly. She knew who it was, though she had only met him formally when she was first hired. But she'd heard Gino Pirelli's voice rumbling through the room more than once since then, usually when he was reaming out some poor office worker for not being quicker or better or something. It was clear to her that the man enjoyed his bullying, and it really didn't matter what the problem was.

Maybe he'll fire me, she thought as she faced him. *Take the decision out of my hands.*

"Yes, sir," she said. "I'm Mary."

His face was a flat slab, with a pushed-in nose and broad forehead and cheeks and a slightly receding chin. He had blank brown eyes. He looked like a classic mob enforcer, a dumb piece of muscle, instead of being the man in charge of the whole shebang.

He seemed slightly irritated, but Mary sensed it wasn't directed at her.

"I need you to come with me, Ms. Patronis," he said.

"I..." She thought about objecting, telling him it was her day off, then decided she'd better not. "Sure."

He led her through the still sparsely populated office. It was early in the morning, which was why she'd thought she could get away with coming in. But it also meant she had probably been the only one available for whatever it was that Mr. Pirelli needed.

She entered the elevator with him with some trepidation, but she needn't have worried. He hardly seemed aware that she was there. He had a scary reputation, but it was also widely rumored that he was madly in love with his wife and never tried to take advantage of any of the women in the office. Indeed, when Jerry Harkins was accused of rape, he'd been gone the next day: not just fired, but really *gone*. No one seemed to know where he went, but there were rumors.

There was a limo at the curb, and Mr. Pirelli ducked into the backseat with surprising agility considering his bulk. Mary hesitated. Should she get in the front seat with the driver, or in back with owner of the company.

"Well, get in, Ms. Patronis," Mr. Pirelli said irritably.

She took a chance and got into the backseat with him, and when he didn't object, she sighed in relief.

They drove through the more prosperous part of town into the zone where there were blocks and blocks of apartment buildings, which Mary knew from doing the paperwork were mostly owned by the corporation.

They stopped at the least dilapidated of the complexes.

"Shall I come in with you, sir?" the driver asked, opening the door. If anything, the man was even bigger than his boss, but with coal-black skin. His suit looked as though it would rip apart, Hulk-like, if he moved too fast in any direction.

"I'll be taking care of this myself," Mr. Pirelli said. "It's my problem."

They walked into the lobby of the building, and Mary saw a pack of young black men in one corner. They rose as if to challenge the white man who'd walked into their territory, but took one look at Mr. Pirelli and backed away.

He got into the elevator and pushed the top button. "When we get to the apartment, I want you to knock on the door. Stand in front of the peephole so Katrina gets a good look at you."

Mary nodded. She had a bad feeling about this.

There was only one door on the top floor, directly across from the elevator. They walked over to it, and while Mary stood in front of it, Mr. Pirelli moved to one side, out of sight.

She knocked timidly and heard someone approach from inside.

"Who is it?" a woman's voice asked, confident, brash, but with an underlying touch of fear.

"My name is Mary Patronis," Mary said. *What was she supposed to say?* It was obvious that her boss wanted inside and was using her as a stalking horse. "I've been going over your rental agreement, and I realized that you forgot to initial something."

"Fuck that," the woman said. "You're lying. Gino took care of all that. I didn't sign shit."

From the corner of her eye, Mary saw Mr. Pirelli moving toward her. Her boss pushed her aside and knocked on the door. It was a solid knock, not overly aggressive, yet something about it gave Mary a chill.

"Let me in, Katrina," he said.

Instead, there came the sound of footsteps retreating.

Mary stood back and watched as the fury grew on Mr. Pirelli's face. He pulled out a keychain and leafed through it briefly, and then seemed to lose patience. Faster than Mary could absorb, he slammed his shoulder into the door, then stepped back and kicked it. It splintered open, and he went inside.

Mary didn't. She stood outside, listening as she heard a sudden scream and a kind of pounding, that, though it didn't shake the building, shook Mary to her core. She felt herself start with every blow, and found herself backing toward the elevator. The screaming grew louder and then stopped.

Mary was all the way in the elevator now, and without thinking, she reached out and pushed the button to the lobby.

She emerged amidst the group of black men, who, a few hours earlier, would have scared her to death. Now she barely noticed them. She walked past the driver, who stared at her, and kept walking. After about thirty minutes of walking, she saw the cathedral in the distance, closer than her apartment. She didn't consciously make the decision to go there, but found herself going through the doors and up the stairs before she could have second thoughts.

Now, she lifted her head, her eyes alighting on the small gargoyle she'd first cleaned. It appeared to be intently watching her.

"May as well get some work done," she said, as if in response to his gaze. "Might as well get my hands dirty—might help me forget."

She went to fill the pail with water, and realized as the water was running that she'd made a decision. She was going to quit her job, no matter the cost. And once she made that decision, a dangerous idea started coming to her.

Whistleblowing, she'd heard, was never rewarded. But was simply quitting enough? Shouldn't she do something about what her employers were doing?

Chapter 18

Jon rose early and got dressed, skipping his morning coffee. He was walking briskly toward the cathedral before he was fully aware that that was his intention.

What am I doing? he asked himself. *In another month, I'm going to be a continent away. I'm done here.*

But his education had never been about degrees or accolades or even his career. Money and status had never motivated him. Curiosity had always driven him, even when it led in unexpected directions. The gargoyles were important, he sensed, though he didn't know why.

And as far as Mary Patronis was concerned, it was even more pointless. Long-distance relationships didn't work; he knew that from hard experience. *Relationships?* He laughed at himself. He had talked to the woman for all of ten minutes, and already he was daydreaming about her. For some reason, she had become important to him. He wanted to get to know her, though he couldn't imagine when he would find the time.

He'd spent most of the night obsessing over her and over the gargoyles until they blended together in his mind, and he somehow knew that they were connected, though he couldn't imagine how.

Why, when, and how: none of it made sense.

Nevertheless, Jon's anticipation grew with every step. He wanted to see Mary again, if only for a second. She didn't even need to converse with him. Just a look would be enough.

He wasn't watching where he was going, so when he sensed movement in front of him, his heart leapt, for he was certain it would be Mary.

Instead, a tall figure in a brown robe stood in front of him. In the daylight, the space within the cowl was dark, and Jon couldn't make out any features.

I didn't know there were any monks here, he thought.

A shiver ran down his spine, for the monk was preternaturally still. Then he turned and walked away so quickly that Jon didn't have a chance to say anything. He hurried to the corner around which the monk had disappeared, but the robed figure was gone. It was an empty corridor, and the storeroom that was Jon's destination was the only room there.

He opened the door the storeroom, holding his breath. A shadow was standing there, not someone tall and dressed in a brown robe, but someone short and round, dressed in priest's vestments. The figure turned around, and Jon realized it was a priest he hadn't met before.

"Yes?" the priest asked, his eyes still fogged by whatever he'd been thinking about.

"I...I'm here to check out the gargoyles," Jon said. "Did you see a monk come in here?"

The priest started, then put an amused expression on his face, an expression that didn't match his eyes. "There are no monks here," he said flatly. "Now, why do you want to check out the gargoyles?"

"I'm doing a doctoral thesis on the cathedral," Jon said. *Have done so already, but I don't need to mention that.* "I just discovered that the gargoyles are numbered. I was thinking perhaps the diocese has information about them?"

"Aren't you one of the construction workers?"

"Maintenance," Jon answered. "It was part of my work/study program."

"I see. What do you need to know?"

"Oh, when they were made. Maybe something about who carved them?"

"You'll have to ask Father Michael," the priest said. "He's in charge of all that."

"And you are?" Jon asked.

"Oh, I apologize," the priest said, stepping forward, hand outstretched. "I'm Father Gregory."

"I didn't know there was another priest here," Jon said. "I've always dealt with Father Michael." This priest was almost the opposite of Father Michael, who was bony and had suspicious eyes. This priest was heavyset and short, with an open face.

"As I said, Father Michael is in charge these days," Father Gregory said. "He doesn't...*acknowledge* me, you might say. I'm sort of retired. But to answer your question about the gargoyles, there is some material in the archives that might be useful." He paused and shrugged. "I'll tell you what. When you're done here, come on down to my office and I'll give you the key. Just don't tell Father Michael, okay?"

"I'll keep it to myself," Jon said, smiling.

Father Gregory turned to leave, then stopped. "Funny you should ask about the gargoyles. You're the second person to become interested in them recently."

"The other being Mary Patronis?"

"Ah, I see you've met her." The priest looked thoughtful. "But then, I guess I shouldn't be surprised. It *is* time."

Time for what? Jon wondered, but before he could ask the question, the priest asked, "Would it be possible for you put the gargoyles back? Once Mary has cleaned them? It's a shame to leave them languishing in here."

Put them back? Jon thought, liking the idea. Until this moment, he hadn't even thought of it.

"I'm just a flunky," Jon said. "My boss, Mr. Hardy, would have to give me the okay. I doubt he'd let me volunteer. He's a pretty hardcore union man."

"Pity," Father Gregory murmured. "Father Michael seems disinclined to ever get them repaired."

They both fell quiet, looking down at the gargoyles. It was sad that other people would never see these magnificent sculptures again.

"I'll see what I can do," Jon said.

"Wonderful!" The priest beamed at him and then gave him directions to his office. "Come by anytime."

"I will. Maybe this afternoon?" Jon put his hand on the gargoyle near the door and felt it move beneath him. He almost cried out. Lifting his hand, he saw only cold, hard unmoving stone.

"I swear they're alive," he said, turning back the priest, but Father Gregory was gone. Strange, he hadn't heard the creak of the door.

Jon contemplated the gargoyles, trying to choose which ones to check first. There were about five of the creatures that were already cleaned: three of the large gargoyles that came from the top of the cathedral, a smaller gargoyle that looked less weathered, as though it came from inside, and of course, the gargoyle he himself had removed.

He pulled out his notebook and started tilting the statues on their sides, writing down the numbers on their bases. The bigger gargoyles' numbers were all written in red paint, which implied they'd probably been installed at around the same time. It looked like the numbers had been applied with spray paint, which meant mid-twentieth century at the earliest.

The smaller gargoyles' numbers were in faded black paint that appeared far older and were hard to read. Jon finished writing down the last of them and sat down near the door, staring at them.

Mary is in danger.

The thought popped into Jon's head. Strange. He hadn't thought it before, but the moment it came to him, he realized it was right.

How do I know that? he wondered. *It's none of my business. I barely know her.*

You must help her.

Jon scrambled to his feet and backed away from the gargoyle he was working on. But the gargoyle, which had a crack running down its furled wings, was lifeless. The voice had come from somewhere else. He glanced around the room, and his gaze fell on the small, polished gargoyle near the door. Its eyes appeared to be gleaming.

I know you can hear me. You must go help Mary, before it is too late.

"What are you?" he asked.

My name is Dominic. I am the gargoyle you see before you.

Jon couldn't help it. He laughed out loud. It was utterly ridiculous. A gargoyle was speaking to him. He pinched himself, though he knew he was awake.

"I'm done here," he said aloud. "This has gone too far. I'm done."

You must *believe me.*

The gargoyle's head turned toward Jon with a grinding sound, and it retracted its broken tongue.

The strength went out of Jon's legs and he sat down heavily, sprawling, staring at the creature. And yet, for some reason, he didn't doubt that what he was seeing and hearing was true. Perhaps he'd picked up the signals subliminally when talking to Mary; perhaps he was going crazy, or perhaps all the legends were true and this cathedral was truly haunted.

But whether it was only his subconscious telling him so or whether it was the gargoyle, he knew Mary was in danger.

"Where is she?" he asked.

She is hiding in the archives.

"Hiding?"

Hurry, Jon. She is in danger as we speak.

Jon remembered Father Gregory's offer to give him the keys to the archives. He struggled to remember the priest's directions to his office. *Follow the stairs below the nave, turn at the first right-hand corridor, two doors down.*

He practically ran out of the storeroom.

"What was all that about a monk?" Pretty asked. "There haven't been monks here for decades."

"Maybe he was imagining things," Grotesque said.

"Well, in the cathedral, imaginary things are usually real," Pretty said.

"What did he see, Alastair?" Dominic asked. "You've explored every nook and cranny of this place, or so you've boasted."

"It's obvious, isn't it?" Grotesque interrupted. "He saw a ghost. One of Alastair's friends, no doubt."

"Is that true?" Dominic cast his voice in the direction of the two ghosts.

Margerie look thoughtful. "It wasn't us," she said.

"Then who was it?" Dominic demanded.

Alastair blinked in and out of view for a few moments, looking uncomfortable. He pulled a handkerchief from his coat and mopped his insubstantial brow.

"All right, Alastair," Dominic said. "Out with it."

"It probably was a ghost," Alastair said, finally. "But there are ghosts…and then there are *ghosts*. You know, the scary kind. The 'Boo! in the graveyard' kind. I think perhaps she saw one of those."

"I've never heard of these ghosts," Dominic said.

"They don't come up into the cathedral very often," Margerie said softly. "The sanctified grounds make them uncomfortable. They stay in the darkness of the catacombs below, nurturing their hate."

"So why would Mary see one?" Pretty asked. "That would seem an ill portent."

Dominic had felt an overwhelming danger surrounding Mary, but until this moment, he had thought it was her mortal life that was in danger. Now he realized that underneath it all, overpowering everything else, was the danger to her soul.

"Who are they?" Dominic asked again. "What do they want?"

Margerie answered. "Alastair here was a philanderer, thoughtless, reckless with women's lives." Alastair looked down as if embarrassed. "Yet he was a good man at heart. He meant no harm. Since he has passed into this purgatory, he has been trying to atone for his sins."

Alastair raised his head, and there was a look of gratitude in his face.

Margerie continued. "When I leapt to my death, it was but a moment of weakness. I despaired. If something had delayed me, or if I had received a kind word from a stranger, I might never have leaped. Both Alastair and I have stayed in this realm because we have felt our work wasn't done, that there was something we yet needed to do before we go to our reward…or our punishment."

Alastair seemed emboldened by her words. "There are other…souls…who have stayed for the opposite reason. They have

91

lingered not to redeem themselves, but to carry on their hate and anger, to look for ways to harm those still living. They are evil spirits, and dangerous."

"Why are they haunting Mary?" Dominic said.

Alastair and Margerie looked at each other, frowning.

"We don't know," Margerie said.

"Well, we need to find out," Pretty said to Dominic. "We're rather limited in what we can do here. Your friends are going to have to do the exploring for us."

"Explore what?" Alastair sounded alarmed.

"You two need to go into the catacombs and find out what's happening."

"We can't go there," Alastair said.

"You can't or you won't?"

Alastair dismissed the question. "Given a will, there is no difference."

"I'll go," Margerie said.

Alastair turned to her, his eyes widening. He put out his hands, which passed through her incorporeal body ineffectually. Then he stood straight.

"No, Margerie...you stay," he said. "I'll go."

It was Margerie's turn to look alarmed. Her eyes widened, and her lips parted as if to protest.

Alastair continued. "If I do not return, defend these good souls, these gargoyles and humans, as best you can."

"We will go together," Margerie objected.

"I have had...dealings with these spirits," Alastair said. "You have said I was a good man, Margerie. I am grateful for that. But there was once a darkness in me you do not know about. I have tried my best to banish it, but when I first became...what I am...I was still very angry." He looked away as if ashamed. "I spent time down there. They know me. I was one of them."

"Will they trust you?" Grotesque asked. "After so much time?"

"They trust no one," Alastair said. "They don't trust each other. They'll be suspicious of me, but they'll wait to see what I do. Evil enjoys the company of evil, and if they believe they can subvert me, then they'll try. I'll play along until I find out what they're up to."

"Seems like a dangerous game," Pretty said. "Careful you don't become one of them once more."

"Aye," Alastair said. "There is that."

Margerie stepped into the glow that was Alastair, and to Dominic's eyes, they appeared to merge.

"Come back to me," she said.

He blinked out of sight, followed a few moments later by Margerie.

Pretty whistled, which made Grotesque break into laughter.

"I thought they hated each other," Pretty said.

"They hate each other so much they spend every moment together," Grotesque replied.

The smaller gargoyle mused. "Strange how this cathedral seems to be the center of an eternal battle between good and evil."

"Yeah, and it's constantly falling apart and under repair," Grotesque answered. "Not much different from the real world, eh?"

Their cheerful banter was for Dominic's sake, he could tell. But it didn't stop him from falling into a deep gloom. Before, when he'd been on the outside of the cathedral, he'd been just as trapped as he was now, but he'd been able to see far distances. Despite the new company, he felt more isolated and helpless than ever before. The inability to move was the true punishment. He felt a surge of frustration pass through him. He longed stand, to walk, to fly.

Dominic felt as though he was rising up on his legs, and for the first time since his creation, spreading his wings. The urge to follow Jon was so strong, he made it several steps before his stone form returned, freezing him in mid-step.

He cried out, but it was only in his mind, for his jaws were once again unmoving, his broken tongue extended.

All in his mind...or so he thought.

There was a sudden silence, and he became aware that Pretty and Grotesque were staring at him in wonder.

"What?" he asked.

"You moved, Dominic," Grotesque said in his rough way, but so softly Dominic could barely hear him.

Pretty joined in, her high voice echoing in the room. "You *moved*."

Chapter 19

Mary rushed into the cathedral hoping she wouldn't run into Father Gregory. There was no way she could hide her panic from him, nor would the good priest be likely to accept any excuses. He'd want to know what had happened, and that would only put him in danger.

They'd known what she'd done before she left the building. She should have known they would catch on fast. When she'd first started working at the real estate office, she'd thought the owners were extraordinarily paranoid. It was only after she'd seen what they were up to that she understood. For some reason they had trusted her, though there was always the threat of retribution if she let anything slip. She figured they thought she was a dumb blonde—good with numbers maybe, but naïve about the world.

Which might have been a fair assessment, considering the trouble she now found herself in.

Mary was in the lobby when her phone rang. It was only luck that Sutherland called her first instead of the security guards.

"What have you done, Mary?" the man said in a low voice, as though afraid he'd be overheard. "Come back now and we'll find a way to explain this."

"Sorry," was all she said before hanging up. She felt sorry for Sutherland, who wasn't a bad man, just a weak one, venal and cowardly. She couldn't blame him too much. She'd been just as venal and cowardly until that morning, when she'd finally screwed up the courage to insert a flash drive into the system and download all the files she'd been saving: only a few months' worth of illegal activity, but still a voluminous amount of information.

She hated to think what they'd do to her boss, but she'd finally decided that the damage these awful men were doing to the poor and innocent outweighed any friendships she had at work. She felt like a rat, but a virtuous rat.

Mary made it to the street before the security guards could stop her, though she heard alarms begin to sound just as she reached the doors. She hurried down the sidewalk, dropping her phone into a corner trash can and ducking down the first side street she reached.

She couldn't go home. She had hoped, after taking the flash drive, that she could decide what to do with it later. Maybe even show up for work a few more times. Find just the right federal law enforcement agency to approach. But those plans had all gone out the window. She didn't trust the city cops, or even the state officials, whom she'd witnessed schmoozing with the head suits of the company.

She walked to the cathedral, deciding not to take a taxi, which might leave a record of where she'd gone.

Once inside, she wondered what she'd been thinking. She should have gone directly to the feds. Surely there was an FBI office in the city. But she was so flustered and scattered that she figured they'd probably think she was a flake, a paranoid conspiracy nut.

She needed a place to rest up and gather her thoughts. Maybe make a few exploratory queries, online and anonymously, if possible. It was Tuesday, she suddenly remembered, and she was certain Father Gregory had mentioned a soup kitchen he volunteered at on that day of the week.

She opened the unlocked door to his office, went to his desk, and opened the top drawer, from which she had seen him extract the key ring. She slid the key card off the loop. Her heart felt like it was in her throat. She could barely breathe. It wasn't just the fear of being caught; it was the betrayal of Father Gregory's trust that really bothered her.

He'll understand, she thought. *Besides, it's his fault I'm even doing this.*

She heard people talking in some of the quiet corners of the cathedral, but the building was so large that she could slip through the shadows and avoid them. Once on the stairs, she wouldn't be able to avoid anyone she might meet, but she was lucky and made it all the way down to the archives without running into anyone. She opened the outer airlock door, and then the inner door. When both doors had clicked shut behind her, she breathed a sigh of relief. She didn't know if there were other keys to the archive, but she'd gotten the distinct impression that other than Father Gregory, few people came down here. It looked exactly the same as it had the day before.

Mary made it as far as the small bed in the little enclave before her tension released. Her body felt as limp as a rag doll's. She flopped onto the bed, intending to close her eyes for a few moments, and fell asleep.

Mary awoke to whispering. She tensed, wondering if she'd been found out. She kept her eyes closed, pretending that she was still sleeping.

"I told you not to follow me," a man's voice said. "It's dangerous."

A woman laughed. "Dangerous, Alastair? I'm a ghost! I wouldn't admit it for a long time, but I remember now. All that happened."

"It is our souls that are in danger, Margerie, not our bodies."

"Even more reason not to hide and cower."

There were a few moments of silence, and then the woman's voice seemed to come from directly above Mary. She tried not to wince, tried not to let on that she was awake. "What's she doing here, Alastair? She doesn't *belong* here."

"Neither do we, Margerie," the male voice answered. There was something strange about their voices, as though they were speaking below Mary's hearing threshold and yet she could hear every word clearly.

"It's *her*," the man, Alastair, continued. "The one Dominic is always talking about."

"Should we tell Dominic?" Margerie asked.

"We must. He needs to know."

"I don't know..." Margerie seemed uncertain. "It's none of our business."

"Nothing is our business," Alastair proclaimed. "Therefore everything is."

Mary groaned as if she was only now waking up. Obviously, she'd been found out. She'd just have to find a way to explain herself. She forced open her eyes.

And saw an empty room.

"Hello?" she called out, craning her neck to see into the other parts of the room. She got up and strode to the center of the room, but there was no one there. A creepy chill ran down her spine, but she shrugged it off. She'd been dreaming. Or she was going crazy.

She reached for her phone to see what time it was, then remembered that she'd trashed it. How much time had passed? She felt the same as when she'd come in. There was no way to gauge the passage of time from how rested, or rather, how tired she still was.

I better return the key card before Father Gregory notices, she thought.

She opened the first door and then turned around, letting it click shut again. She began looking for something that would keep the locks from clicking home. She experimented with some folded paper across the locks and satisfied herself that it would keep the locks from taking hold. She closed one door and then did the same thing to the second door. She crept up the steps. There was a deep silence in the air, as if the cathedral was slumbering.

Mary reached Father Gregory's office and put the key card back, then hurriedly rushed back down to her hiding place. The papers had held, and she was able to get back into the room, letting the locks take hold on her way in. If anyone came down here with the key, she was caught, but she didn't think she'd need that much time, just enough to upload the information on the computer and send it to the proper authorities.

She sat at the desk and turned on the computer, and her heart fell. It was asking for a password.

Chapter 20

Talking gargoyles.

The moment Jon left the storeroom, the whole thing seemed ridiculous. He stopped and leaned against the hallway wall, closing his eyes and taking a deep breath. *I've been working too hard. My dissertation, the cathedral...and now this.*

Whatever this *is. An illusion, a mental breakdown, something...whatever it is, it isn't supernatural. It can't be. No such thing as "supernatural."*

He pushed away from the wall. It didn't matter. He had planned on visiting the archives anyway, so either Mary would be there or she wouldn't. He trudged down the stairs, his head down, for once not seeing the glorious colors of the stained glass or the fine architectural features. Instead, he was trying to cast his thoughts into the future, to his upcoming trip to Spain, where all of this wouldn't matter.

Just go back to the dorm, he thought. *Leave it be.*

Jon reached the nave and looked up into the vastness of the dome above. It was as if shadows had formed in corners he'd never seen before. As if the air had thickened with something as thick and choking as smoke, but unseen. As if the cathedral was a creature coming alive, instead of the quiet, contemplative refuge he'd always thought it.

He shook his head and continued down the stairs. He'd never been below the ground level of the cathedral before, and now he wondered why. He'd been so interested in the artistic features of the building that he'd never examined the foundations. Which was strange, since the foundations were important. It had just never come up.

I'm an art major, not an architecture major.

Father Gregory's office was two floors down. Jon suddenly realized he didn't know if he'd gone two floors or one. He turned off into the hallway, went two doors down, and opened the door.

It was a storage unit, filled with boxes of paper and broken or outdated office machinery.

He closed the door. Another floor, then.

Jon sensed something move behind him, and he whirled around. The hallway lights were out farther down, so he wasn't sure if he'd seen a hooded figure move across the hallway or just imagined it. *Curious. What's down there?*

He turned that direction.

"Mr. Williams?" he heard someone say behind him. He turned to see Father Gregory approaching him, his hand held out. "Are you lost?"

"Apparently," Jon said. "I've never been down here before."

"I was coming to look for you when I saw you coming out of the storeroom. My office is another floor down. Come along, we'll get you a key. In fact, why don't I just take you down there?"

"That would be great," Jon answered. He meant it, too. These subterranean corridors were spooky. Having the cheerful priest along seemed like a great idea.

Should I tell him about the gargoyles? he wondered, then realized how crazy that was. Father Gregory might deal with the realm of the spiritual and the unseen, but most priests that Jon had met were pretty down to earth.

They continued down another flight of stairs. The next hallway was brightly lit as well as carpeted. It seemed almost homey. The priest's office added to that impression, with its couch and cushions and cluttered desk and overflowing bookshelves.

Father Gregory opened the top drawer of the desk, removed a set of keys, and jangled them at Jon with a big smile. "You're going to love this," he said. "Go on, I'll follow you."

The atmosphere grew dank and cool as they descended, but Jon was indeed fascinated by the antiquity of the stairs, with their worn grooves, and the heavy wooden doors of the occasional rooms they passed, with ornate carvings that he would have loved to examine closer.

I've only touched the surface of this cathedral, Jon thought. *Literally as well as figuratively.*

He turned to say as much to the priest, but there was no one there. How long since he'd heard the Father's footsteps? Or heard him speak?

Jon continued on, figuring that Father Gregory would catch up. He hadn't gone very far before he started regretting the decision. There were corridors branching off in every direction; some of them had stairs in them, and Jon couldn't be absolutely sure he was still in the main stairway.

He almost turned around. The bare bulbs running along the ceiling were flickering as if they wanted to blink out. Jon wasn't sure he could handle that. He'd always been a little leery of the dark. He suspected the dark down here would be darker than anything he'd ever experienced.

The echoes of his footsteps both preceded and followed him down the corridor. The lights seemed dimmer, as if begrudging him their glow. He coughed and felt phlegm rising in his throat, as if the cool dankness was loosening the fluids in his lungs.

Maybe I should wait for Father Gregory, he thought. *Or go back.*

The idea of having come all this way and then turning around was unappealing.

Jon picked up his pace, almost slipping on the slick stone a few times.

He turned a sharp corner. A wall of white greeted him, textured and gnarled. He put out his hand and then retracted it quickly. Despite the moist air, the surface of the white thing he'd touched felt dry and old.

He stepped back in alarm. It wasn't a wall, but a room filled with bones, stacked so high and deep that they had melded together.

How could I have missed these? he wondered. *I read everything I could about the cathedral, and I never knew it had catacombs!*

He continued on, and another room opened on his left, also filled with bones. One more level down, individual crypts started to appear on either side, open, each about the size of small chest, filled with the jumbled bones of ancient burials. Jon stopped and reached into one where he saw a glint of yellow. It was a necklace, and the gold was as shiny as the day it had been made.

What other treasures are there down here? How I would love to study them! Jon thought.

I'm leaving in a week, he reminded himself. *It's too late.*

Strangely, instead of the bones creeping him out, they somehow put everything into perspective for Jon. This was an old building, and these were the remains of generations of the devoted. It was all natural.

He heard voices in the distance, below him. Had Father Gregory somehow gotten ahead of him? He continued onward, and the voices he heard began to rise in volume. It was a man and a woman. As he came closer, he realized the man sounded threatening and the woman scared.

"Let go of me!" the woman cried.

Jon descended one last sharp turn. The voices fell away. Mary was up against a door, not one of the old wooden doors that had so fascinated Jon on his way down, but a modern, almost high-tech-looking door. Father Michael was leaning against her, his forearm across her neck as if holding her in place.

They were both looking at him as if he was an apparition.

Chapter 21

Father Michael was annoyed. He made his way down to his office, paying little attention to his surroundings.

Am I being punished? he wondered.

It felt more and more like he didn't know what was going on in his own cathedral. The Catholic Conservation Committee was apparently assigning volunteers to clean the gargoyles without asking him. Not only that, but some of the removed gargoyles were being put back into place without permission.

He'd been assigned to shut down this place quietly and efficiently.

"Do it slowly, so no one notices," Cardinal O'Malley had ordered. "Let it fall apart, but not so that it hurts anyone. Just keep it safe until it's so dilapidated that our opponents will have no choice but to let us tear it down, historical value or not. The city block that old dinosaur is situated on is so valuable that we could build ten modern cathedrals to take its place."

Father Michael had felt proud of the assignment at first, but as time passed, he realized he was in purgatory, waiting for a structure that had lasted through two hurricanes and an earthquake to fall apart by itself.

What did I do wrong?

Cardinal O'Malley reassured him that he had done nothing wrong—whenever he could get through to his superior, which was rarer and rarer these days. "You're the only man for the job," his boss said with that Irish cheerfulness that was his trademark. "Hang in there, Mike. We'll get you your dream assignment next time."

When the gargoyle had fallen off the façade and killed that civilian, it had appeared the gig was up and that they'd really have to get serious about fixing up the cathedral. But it had turned out that the man was a trespasser on the property, so there was no liability by the archdiocese. Indeed, the incident had allowed Father Michael to remove more of the gargoyles, of which Cardinal O'Malley was completely supportive. "We can sell them," the cardinal said. "Some of my richer patrons will pay big money for them."

Father Michael frowned. The cardinal hadn't come out and said that he was pocketing the money, but the implication was clear, as was the suggestion that no one would notice if Father Michael took a little for himself.

In his more reflective moments, Father Michael knew himself to be a petty man, but he wasn't dishonest. He tended to lose his temper over small things, perhaps, and to be a little bit of a grump. He was also a man who had lust in his heart. Most of the time he could control it, but once or twice he had slipped.

Maybe that's why I'm here, he suddenly thought as he opened the door to his office. *They know*. He shook off the thought. *I'm not as bad as the previous priest. Nowhere near as bad as him.*

His top desk drawer was open. Father Michael didn't remember leaving it like that. In fact, he was a little anal about such things as open drawers and doors, and lights left on, and garbage overflowing trash cans. He moved quickly to the other side of the desk and sat in his chair, which seemed positioned lower than usual.

The keys were still there. He sighed in relief.

Maybe it's time I put them in the safe, he thought. It seemed like things were getting moved around, though he couldn't figure out how it was happening. They had very few visitors these days.

Maybe it's that woman, that Mary Patronis. I don't trust her.

He'd checked on her work and had been impressed, despite himself, by how well the gargoyles cleaned up. But it seemed sort of pointless, since they were never going to be put back. Or so he had thought and intended.

That morning, he'd caught Hardy and his crew putting back one of the gargoyles. It had been a massive, ugly thing, really evil looking. It looked as fresh as if it had been carved the day before, frighteningly lifelike. The other gargoyles nearby looked almost quaint in comparison, as if they could be sold in a gift shop. This one looked like it belonged on the cover of a cheap horror novel.

"What are you doing?" he asked the workers. "Who gave you permission to do this?"

"Well, boss, we had a little extra time today, and we thought we'd put some of these bad boys back, you know, make it all look nice," Hardy said. "We ain't charging you for it."

"I don't care," Father Michael said. "You need to ask first."

"Why?" Hardy said. There was a defiant look on his face, and the men behind him were openly glaring at Father Michael, as if they hated him.

Father Michael didn't answer immediately. Hardy had been here before him and seemed to have a lot of support among the Catholic Conservation Committee. The priest had the power to fire the man and his crew, but not without repercussions.

"Please ask me next time," he'd finally muttered.

But the very next day, he caught them at it again: installing another gargoyle that he didn't recognize. They were dragging it out of a storeroom that Father Michael didn't remember ever having seen before. How was that possible? He was sure he'd explored every inch of the cathedral.

Behind the men, the door was ajar, and Michael could see that the room was packed with gargoyles. "Are these the same gargoyles that were removed before?" he asked.

Hardy looked away, but not before the priest saw the evasiveness in his eyes. "Before your time, Father Michael. These have been here a long time."

"But are they being put back where they came from originally?"

"Don't matter, does it?" Hardy growled.

"Well, yes, it does matter. These gargoyles were meant to be useful, you know. They were designed for their positions to drain the maximum amount of water."

105

"Don't worry, boss." The foreman put his hand on the gargoyle as if he was stroking a pet. "This fellow will do the job."

Father Michael walked away frustrated. He'd have to find a logical reason for the gargoyles not to be reinstalled. He couldn't let anyone know what he was really up to. He couldn't allow that.

There was a framed picture of a gargoyle on the wall of the office, which Father Michael hated but hadn't felt like he could remove. It had once graced the cover of a book about gargoyles and was a gift from the publisher. Michael frowned. It was an impressive picture, and the gargoyle looked threatening in a medieval way. But not completely evil.

Not like the ones he'd just seen.

He opened his office drawer and picked up the book.

Hard to believe now that he'd once been a believer. Not just in Catholic or Christian traditions, but in all things unseen, the supernatural, the mystical. It was all gone by the time he arrived at the cathedral. The priest who had his job before him, a wizened old man who was retiring to meditate on a mountaintop or some such nonsense, had reverently handed him a small book.

"This goes with the job," Father Jonathan had said. "It goes with the cathedral. Believe its contents or not, it's up to you. Frankly, I believe it, and I'm glad that I won't be here when the day comes."

Father Michael had looked through the small volume, with its scribbled and crabbed handwriting, and rolled his eyes. First of all, most of the contents were heresy that the Church would have frowned upon, to say the least. Secondly, it seemed to be magical mumbo jumbo about how criminals had been turned into gargoyles, to serve in purgatory, to protect the cathedral, and how if they did their job, they would be released from their limbo.

There was a prophecy that the cathedral would one day be the scene of a great battle between good and evil, and that the gargoyles would be released to fight the invading demons. There was even a prayer included that was supposed to do the job.

Total nonsense. Father Michael had almost destroyed the book, but in the end had simply squirrelled it away in a bottom drawer of his desk, where it had slowly gotten covered by out-of-date receipts and useless paraphernalia.

There had been a lot about the gargoyles in the book, if he remembered rightly. He leafed through it now, but still couldn't make sense of it. Spells and magic, that's all it was.

Gargoyles were functional, as he always tried to point out to the Catholic Conservation Committee, but the job could be done better by more modern means. But as at least one member of the committee always pointed out, they were symbolic too. They were supposed to protect the cathedral and those who prayed within it from evil.

Damned if he could remember any gargoyles looking like what Hardy and his men were installing, either in real life or in books. They would have had to have been taken out in the early years, before good records were kept. But if there were any documents about them, they would be in the archives.

Father Michael grabbed the keys out of the drawer and left the office, heading down into the catacombs. He had always avoided them as much as possible. His predecessor had installed the climate-controlled room, which was a shame, because if the Conservation Committee couldn't prove something existed, they couldn't protect it. As it was, Father Michael had to account for each and every change he made to the façade.

He'd only visited the archives once before. Truth was, death scared him. His least favorite duty as a parish priest—before he'd been relegated to administrative duties—had been officiating at funerals. He hated the finality of it all, the grieving relatives, and the creepy graveyards. Truth was, he wasn't very good with people, living or dead. His duties in an almost empty cathedral were a perfect match for his temperament.

He passed the bone rooms without looking, keeping his eyes on the floor. He was so tall that he had to hunch over to get through some of corridors, but that wasn't too much of a chore since that was his natural posture, learned when he was young and seemingly bumping his head against every overhead obstacle.

When he heard a noise up ahead, he stopped dead in his tracks, taking in a deep breath that he held as he listened. He had to almost remind himself to breathe again.

There were stories about these catacombs.

Father Michael didn't believe in ghosts. He didn't believe in anything supernatural anymore, even all the Catholic mumbo jumbo. But damned if he was going to tell anyone that—he was too old to start a new career.

Despite himself, he clutched his rosary and went forward slowly, poking his head around the last corner.

A woman was closing the door to the archives, whistling to herself. She had a backpack on and was holding a water battle with one hand. The door didn't close all the way, and he saw that she'd propped a rock between it and the jam.

"What are you doing here?" he asked sharply.

The woman turned and let out a small shriek, dropping the plastic bottle, which bounced on the stone floor and splashed water over her shins.

"Oh, my God! You frightened me," she said.

"You're that girl the Conservation Committee sent, aren't you?" Father Michael asked.

Relief came over her face, as if she was grateful that he recognized her. But there was something a little off about her expression, as if she'd been caught doing something she shouldn't be doing.

"Yes, thanks for remembering," she said. "I...uh...was just doing some examining of the records. To see, you know, if we were taking care of everything."

"The chairman is a perfectionist, isn't he?" Father Michael said, forcing himself to smile. "Remembers everything, John Hoskins does."

"He's a bit of a pill," she agreed.

He kept staring at the woman until her smile slipped. She shrugged. "There is no John Hoskins, is there?" she asked resignedly.

"The chairperson is an old biddy named Shelby, and she can barely remember her own name."

"Look, I need a place to hide," she said, and it was clear that she was being sincere for the first time. "I've gotten into trouble at my job.

I found out I was working for some people who were doing illegal things. *Immoral* things."

The word "immoral" was obviously supposed to gain Father Michael's sympathy, but he felt nothing. "How did you even know about this place?" he asked. "Who told you about it?"

The woman started to answer, then seemed to think twice, as if she was afraid of getting someone in trouble. "No one," she said. "I just stumbled upon it."

"And the keys?" He held up the keychain, wondering himself how she could have possibly found them.

"It was unlocked," she said unconvincingly. It might have been possible, if unlikely, that one of the doors had accidentally remained ajar, but it was impossible that both could have been. The whole purpose of the arrangement, after all, was to keep the moisture out of the archives. It would be beyond neglectful for anyone to have left both doors open. Besides, Father Michael hadn't loaned the keys out to anyone, including anyone on the Conservation Committee.

Father Michael approached the woman, stopping mere inches away, using his height to loom over her, which he had long ago discovered could be intimidating to some women.

She was beautiful, though she tried to hide it under baggy clothing and minimal makeup. Her blonde hair was thick, and cut short. Her blue eyes were clear and deep, like two pools of water he could dive into. Her long nose only served to show how perfect the rest of her features were.

Father Michael started getting uncomfortably hard. He was grateful for once for his voluminous robes.

She tried to move away from him, and without thinking, he put his forearm against her throat, holding her in place.

"Let go of me!" she cried out.

Father Michael suddenly wondered if he'd gone too far. What would she say when she was let go? There had been hints about his behavior before, though no one had ever accused him formally. *Is this the end of my career?*

Before he could decide what to do, he heard the sound of footsteps. At the end of the corridor, a man appeared. They stared at each for a moment. It was that annoying college student, Father Michael realized, the one they'd foisted upon him to assign to the maintenance crew.

"What's going on?" Jon Williams asked.

Chapter 22

"What's going on?" Jon's voice sounded calm to his own ears. Which amazed him, because what he really wanted to do was charge the priest and throw him down the stairs.

The priest stepped back, letting Mary go. He had a hangdog expression, as if he wanted to lower his head even further from his usual stoop. As he leaned against the wall, his robes bulged outward at the waist, and it was clear he had an erection.

Mary stood there as if not quite sure she was really free, then slid along the wall a few inches in Jon's direction, and then turned and practically ran to him. She went past him as if she was going to keep going, but then stopped and turned.

"She was trespassing," Father Michael said, straightening up defiantly. "And so are you, young man."

"We have permission to be here," Jon said.

"I doubt it," the priest said. "How do you even know about this place? How did you find your way here without getting lost? How did *she* get a key to the archives?"

Jon turned his head slightly to look at Mary. "Father Gregory?" he whispered. She nodded.

"As it happens, we got permission from Father Gregory," he said out loud. "In fact, he was behind me just a few moments ago. I'm sure he'll be along any moment. He'll be curious to know what's happening here."

Father Michael's face went blank, and then he started laughing, as if he'd just heard the most unexpected and humorous thing ever.

"Oh, I'm sure," he said. "Maybe he's already here! Shall we check?" He turned and motioned for them to follow. He went down the small staircase to the next level and looked up at them expectantly. Jon and Mary exchanged glances, as if both were wondering if they were being led into a trap.

The priest was about five inches taller than Jon, who was nearly six feet. But Jon probably weighted thirty pounds more than the other man. Jon didn't think he had much to worry about if the confrontation became physical. But there was something about the way the priest was acting, as if he knew something they didn't.

Jon looked toward Mary again, but she was already stepping beside him. "Might as well find out what he's up to," she said.

Previously, while the air had felt somewhat dank and cool, the walls and floors had been dry. Now Jon began to see droplets of water hanging from the ceiling. One of them fell on his face as he was looking up and streamed into the corner of his mouth. He wiped it away hastily, not wanting to taste it.

Mary lost her footing beside him, and he grabbed her arm, holding her up. When she was steady again, she didn't let go. Her hand traveled down his arm and grasped his. After that, while still conscious of everything else going on around them, Jon was hyperaware of that hand clutching his. It was as if they were communicating their fears and hopes and were both strengthened by the exchange.

"I've been down here before," Mary said. "There's nothing down here."

"Nothing alive," Father Michael agreed, suddenly stopping. There was a small crypt to one side with a skeleton inside it. The black robes it was clothed in were falling apart, but there were still remnants of fabric left. The bony hands clasped on its chest were clutching a crucifix. The cross was upside down, Jon noticed, trying to make sense of it.

But even before the priest announced it, Jon knew. From the tightness of Mary's grasp, she had guessed it to.

"*This* is Father Gregory!" the priest said triumphantly. "Personally, I think this foul pederast doesn't belong here on hallowed ground, but that was when the Church was still denying such things...and I suppose it would be too embarrassing to move him somewhere else now. Too much explaining to do. Best to just hope no one remembers or notices."

"The Father Gregory we're talking about had a bit more flesh on his bones than this," Jon said.

"*Considerably* more flesh," Mary agreed.

Father Michael nodded his head. "Yes, I've seen old black and white photos of the bastard, and he was a hefty man. My understanding is that there wasn't a single one of the seven deadly sins that Gregory—I won't call him Father—didn't indulge in." He reached out and touched the upside-down crucifix with a frown, then apparently decided to let it be.

"So you're saying we saw a ghost?" Mary said.

"I don't believe in ghosts," Jon said.

"Neither do I, and yet I keep seeing them," Father Michael said. "Look, I know you think I'm a bastard and a hard case, but I'm trying to hold this cathedral together, and at the same time, make sure it is safe. You can't just be wandering around here without permission."

"Perhaps not," Jon said. "But attacking a young women seems a little over the top. If Mary here presses charges against you, I'll testify that it looked as if you were meaning to attack her. And I don't just mean physically."

Father Michael, who until that moment had seemed to think he had the upper hand, nearly collapsed at that. His tall frame seemed to fold up on itself, and his head seemed to bend down to his waist. "Please..." he whispered. "Please don't do that. I have a problem, I admit, but I have always controlled it, and I would have controlled it this time, I swear. I swear upon all the souls in these catacombs."

Jon didn't believe him, nor was he inclined to give the priest the benefit of the doubt, so he was surprised when Mary spoke up.

"I think we can let it go," she said. "But in exchange, I need a place to stay. I've been using the small bed in the archives. I will be very careful to leave everything else alone. I promise."

"Are you sure?" Jon asked. She was still holding his hand, and she squeezed it hard. There was a look on her face that seemed to implore him not to ask too many questions.

Father Michael raised his head and halfway straightened up. "If you promise not to touch anything, I think that might be acceptable."

They stood there in silence for a few moments, and then Father Michael motioned that he'd like to get by them. They squeezed against the wall as he went by. He didn't look back until he reached the corner; then, at the last moment, he stopped and turned around.

He looked concerned. "If I were you, I wouldn't be talking to Father Gregory. The stories about him...he was a truly evil man."

Then he lurched out of view.

Mary finally let go of Jon's hand, and he felt a immediate pang of loss. Holding her hand had felt comfortable and natural. It was this standing apart, as if they were strangers, that felt wrong.

But we are *strangers,* he thought. *We barely know each other.*

"You were coming down to use the archives, I assume?" she asked awkwardly.

He nodded.

"Let me show you the way in." She turned without another word and started up the hallway, leading him toward where they had first met.

Chapter 23

It is time. Father Gregory sent the message to his followers, knowing they would be waiting for him by the time he arrived.

He could've flashed to the meeting room instantly, but he preferred to walk, to pretend for just a little longer that he was still alive. His body was an illusion when he wanted it to be, but unlike most ghosts, his body was also corporeal when he needed it to be. He believed, because of this, that he wasn't really a ghost, but more the manifestation of his Masters' wishes and needs.

Still, he retained the memories of the man he'd once been.

There had always been men like him in the orders, and whenever they were discovered, they were shunted aside, given meaningless duties, made to feel unwelcome in hopes that they would leave. But they weren't exposed, and they weren't cast out.

Father Gregory had never been caught in his lifetime, and thus had continually risen in the hierarchy until he'd been given control over this prestigious cathedral. There, in the catacombs, he had met his Masters, who'd been waiting a long time for someone like him. They promised him not some ethereal afterlife that Father Gregory no longer believed in—or if he still believed, was now sure was a place he would never reach.

No, they promised to grant him eternal consciousness, now and forever. They would give him power upon the world, both seen and unseen. He would be their favorite, their lieutenant, their power upon this Earth and over its denizens.

If he but served them.

He wasn't naïve. He knew his Masters had made such promises millions of times to all manner of the fallen.

But he also knew how valuable the cathedral was, how the Masters hungered for dominion over what had once been the most blessed of places. All over the world, the same offer was made, and had been made from the beginning of time, and because of man's failures and weakness, evil always found a way to enter.

But never like this. Never before had such a consecrated and hallowed ground been so vulnerable; never had so holy a spot become available.

To walk the hallways and remember when he'd been in charge of this magnificent cathedral filled Father Gregory with nostalgia. In his day, the cathedral had been busier, of course. People had thronged churches and synagogues and mosques back then, and they had believed, truly believed, which was why it had taken him so long to get his appointed task done.

Just as well, he thought. *Now is the perfect time; now we have the perfect sacrificial victims.*

The world outside was chaotic, filled with moral decay and ethical ambiguity. Even the members of the religious order he had infiltrated were doubters in this modern age. They wouldn't know what to make of the invasion until it was too late.

They'd sent a caretaker who was a nonbeliever, though Father Gregory had advised his Masters against approaching him. Not so much because he thought Father Michael would resist the enticements—which was the reason he gave—but because he didn't like the idea of sharing the power that would come on that fateful day when the church became a portal for his Masters to use to cross into this world.

His Masters had waited a long time for this day. Once, the cathedral and others like it had been a bulwark against their kind, protecting humanity, and in return, humanity had at least professed to believe in their Maker and His heaven.

Now? No one believes anything.

Too late, humanity and the unbelievers and sinners who were now the majority would realize that everything they discounted was true, that there was true evil, and that the Masters had long wanted to occupy this world, and only the great religions and their adherents had kept them away.

It was ironic that in this modern age, those who professed to believe the most in righteousness were the worst of all. The so-called fundamentalists lived more for empty words than the true virtues the founders of their religions had preached.

The cathedral was undefended by any human who mattered or who had power to stop the Masters.

But even more importantly, the sanctified ground was unshielded by the gargoyles, those protectors that had once graced its walls, which modern man made the mistake of believing were purely symbolic. Father Gregory had started the decline of this grand old cathedral while he was still living. When he'd died and those he had terrorized finally came forward, his evil had been exposed. The cathedral was discredited and attendance dropped to numbers that could no longer provide for its upkeep.

Short-term caretakers, such as the Conservation Committee, had short-term and parsimonious small minds, and they had continued the cathedral's decline, and now, as the gargoyles were removed, one by one, the cathedral was at last ready to be transformed, transmuted into a place not of good, but of evil. Without the protective gargoyles, the church was undefended both from within and without.

It was time.

Father Gregory entered the dark room, but to him the blackness didn't matter. He could see his followers within, arrayed around the old table. Hardy had been the first. Father Gregory had fed the man the wiggling piece of a Master that had been sent across, and the man had fallen to the floor, squirming, frothing at the mouth. He'd gasped for breath, his eyes bugging out, his legs thrashing. His bowels had voided, filling the room with stench.

And then he'd arisen, and was one of them. One by one, the others in the maintenance crew had been turned, and slowly but surely, they had weakened and damaged the gargoyles until they could be removed.

It was surprisingly easy. The gargoyles were asleep, or perhaps even dead. There were not enough believers within the cathedral walls to keep them awake, to maintain their vigilance.

All but a few.

Those gargoyles Father Gregory had left for last.

"Are we ready?" he asked as he walked in the door. His followers had let their true natures manifest within the meeting room. Tentacles sprouted from their faces, and instead of hands, claws emerged from their robes, and beneath the robes, sharp hooves were visible.

"We have installed half of the gargoyles," Hardy said. "We can do the rest whenever you give the orders. We are short-handed, however. Our last recruit failed. Kip didn't come back."

Father Gregory frowned in displeasure. Not all the potential candidates accepted the small, slimy pieces of the Masters. Some goodness remained in them. They spit up the bit of tentacle, and with it, most of their insides.

"What about Jon?" Ollie Simmons asked. "The little prick could be useful for once."

Hardy answered before Father Gregory could. "Wouldn't work. Jon doesn't have a mean bone in his body."

"He doesn't have to know," Ollie insisted. "Just order him to help."

"He'd know something was wrong," Father Gregory said. "He'd feel it. He's a good boy. In fact, I have other plans for him, and for the girl. We need a couple of sacrificial lambs, and it seems to me they fit the bill. They are innocents, believers in their hearts. Not only that, but they are both inside the cathedral at this moment. We just need to keep them here while we finish the configuration.

"Get going, boys," he finished. "The time has come to end this thing and bring about that for which we have worked."

The men stood up as one, and as one they turned to the creatures behind them. They had the appearance of gargoyles, but they were demons. It was ironic that the whole purpose of gargoyles was to appear to be demons, and yet their job was the opposite of demons', and here were real demons pretending to be gargoyles. Their job was not to protect this place, but to usher in the forces of the underworld.

"We can finish tonight," Hardy said. "We installed the harder-to-reach gargoyles first. We only have a few easy ones left."

"Finish by midnight, and I will deliver the victims to the altar," Father Gregory said.

Hardy nodded. He motioned and the "gargoyles" that until now had been hidden in the darkness emerged, slithering, crawling, slouching forward, following the things that had once been men but were now the puppets of the Masters. Their skin wasn't hard and dry but glistening with slime, leaving a trail of ooze upon the stone floor. Their teeth were real, made for rending, and with their wings, they could fly. They weren't protectors, they were hunters, and they would herd the humans into the cathedral until they were needed for sacrifice, and they would keep them there.

By tomorrow morning, the Masters will be here, on Earth, Father Gregory thought. *I will earn my reward at last.*

Chapter 24

Now that they were alone, Mary and Jon suddenly fell silent, as if unsure what to say to each other. Each wondered how much the other believed what Father Michael had told them. Jon had no doubt it was true, but he also knew how crazy it sounded.

He looked over at Mary. She was as beautiful as he remembered, though she seemed to have lost a little of her confidence. That vulnerability made him want to protect her, to take her hand again and never let go.

"Why did you come down here?" Mary finally asked as they approached the door to the archives.

Jon thought about how the gargoyle, Dominic, had told him that Mary was in danger. Then realized how crazy that sounded, too.

"There's something weird about the gargoyles," he replied.

She snorted a little. "You can say that again."

He ventured a smile, and she burst out laughing. He joined her. All the tension, within and without Jon, seemed to vanish. Moments before, the cathedral had felt threatening and Mary standoffish. Now it was if they were old friends.

She pushed the door open, and he saw now that it was thick and made of metal. There was a small room behind it, and another door that looked exactly like the first. Mary carefully closed the first door before she went to open the second. Jon saw that she had duct-taped the doors' locking mechanisms so that they wouldn't latch. Even so, the doors closed with solid thunks.

Beyond was a room full of shelves, from floor to ceiling. After the humidity of the corridors outside, the dryness within was instantly palpable. Jon walked over to one of the shelves and picked up an unbound pile of papers. There was beautiful handwriting on the yellowed pages. A small piece of the corner of the top page broke off and floated to the floor, and he put the manuscript back gently.

The scholar within Jon was flabbergasted, first that this archive existed at all and second that he'd never heard of it until recently. He wondered how many Catholic scholars knew about it and what would happen if it became common knowledge.

He felt possessive of it all of a sudden, as if he didn't want to share. Let him have a head start investigating all this and his career might be made. He started to wonder how easy it would be to get a refund on his plane ticket to Spain, and whether the Sagrada Familia Foundation would be willing to wait for him.

"Good stuff?" Mary asked, and he realized she was looking at him intently.

"Marvelous stuff," he said. "I can't believe these idiots have kept it all secret. Who knows what we might find here?"

"The Fathers don't seem very generous, do they?" she said. At the mention of the priests, they both fell silent again.

"You don't really think we saw Father Gregory's ghost, do you?" Jon asked quietly. "It must be some kind of prank."

"I would have thought so, a few months ago. Before I started hearing voices." Mary grimaced as she realized how that sounded. "I mean, I could be crazy, I guess. But I don't think so. I think this cathedral is...haunted."

"The gargoyles..." Jon said, and broke off to see what her reaction would be.

She nodded firmly. "Yes, especially the gargoyles. Like my little friend upstairs."

"I know what you mean," Jon said. "It seems like they've been talking to me, too. I've taken to giving them names, even."

He turned toward the stacks of books, lifted one up, read the title, and put it back. It was hopeless. There was no way he'd find what he needed.

"What's the matter?" Mary asked.

"I was hoping to look up the history of the gargoyles," Jon said. "When they were installed, who carved them, what they were supposed to represent at the time. That kind of thing." He raised his hands and turned a full circle with a helpless look on his face. "How on earth am I supposed to find anything?"

"Father Gregory—or whoever that was—showed me something," Mary said. She walked toward a doorway that Jon only now noticed. She turned on a switch. Unlike in the first room, the lighting here was modern. The room was mostly clean, with manuscripts piled neatly on a long table near a computer. It was an older laptop, but Jon had worked on one like it before, and when he turned it on, he quickly found his way around.

There...*A Map of Gargoyles*. He pulled it up onto the screen, and there was an overhead diagram of the cathedral, including the numbered placement of all the sculptures. He pulled his notebook out of his back pocket and compared the two diagrams.

Weird. There was a pattern there he hadn't noticed before. He looked around and found an outdated monstrosity of a printer on the floor under the table. He hooked it up and pressed "copy."

As the page started slowly rolling out—it wasn't a laser print, but an old-fashioned dot matrix printer—he looked around for a ruler.

"Look for something with a straight edge," he said to Mary.

Mary walked around the perimeter of the room, then darted into the manuscript room, coming back a few moments later with a book that looked only a few years old, or at the very least, from the current century. It was a picture book of gargoyles, with a sculpture Jon recognized from the cathedral on the cover. It was the gargoyle Jon had always thought of as Grotesque.

"That'll do it," he said. He pulled the paper out of the printer the instant it stopped chattering and laid it flat on the table. He took the edge of the book and drew a series of lines between the points of the cathedral where he knew gargoyles had already been removed. There were ten points: the five points of a star and its five inner vertices. All of them were now empty. The last one removed had been the small gargoyle Jon had helped take down and that Mary had named Dominic.

"Wow," he said, as the pattern emerged. When he was done, he held it up to Mary.

"A pentagram?" she said. "What does it mean?"

"Traditionally," Jon mused, "I believe that it has been used to keep an evil spirit trapped...a demon, or even the devil. If the pentagram is broken, the evil entity is released."

"Broken?" Mary said, looking at the map. "Hell, the gargoyles on the points are completely gone!"

Jon stared at the map a while longer. He checked to see if the computer was connected to the Internet and was pleased to see that it was. He looked up "pentagram," and began researching the entries on cathedrals. Mary was standing behind him, and she put her hand on his shoulder. He started in surprise, but she didn't seem to notice. As he browsed, he was intensely conscious of her breath on his neck.

"Hold it, did you see this?" she asked, and then read from the screen. "If you measure the length of the nave, and the choir and the transepts of the Chartres Cathedral, they are multiples of the Golden Mean. Wasn't this cathedral a copy of Chartres?"

"Somewhat," Jon said, feeling slightly offended at the word "copy." It had been the starting point, but the American architects had put their own spin on things.

"The Golden Mean," he repeated. "I know this...1.618."

She gave him an admiring glance. He shrugged. "I'm an art major. You don't study Leonardo da Vinci without learning the Golden Ratio."

She leaned over him and typed in "da Vinci," and he got a deep whiff of her, and it made him dizzy. The first picture that popped up was the Vitruvian Man.

"Looks like someone trapped within a pentagram, doesn't it?" Jon mused.

"Listen to this," Mary said. "The pentagram can also be used to keep demons out. So..." She moved the drawn pentagram over the diagram of the cathedral. "It protects the cathedral from evil. That was no doubt the original intent."

123

"How about this? " Jon said. "This is from Wikipedia. Goethe's description in *Faust* of trapping Mephistopheles:

"Mephistopheles:
I must confess, my stepping o'er
Thy threshold a slight hindrance doth impede;
The wizard-foot [Drudenfuss] doth me retain.

Faust:
The pentagram thy peace doth mar?
To me, thou son of hell, explain,
How camest thou in, if this thine exit bar?
Could such a spirit aught ensnare?

Mephistopheles:
Observe it well, it is not drawn with care,
One of the angles, that which points without,
Is, as thou seest, not quite closed."

"So the pentagram must be broken for a demon to be able to enter?" Mary asked.

"That's the way I read it," Jon said. "But what puzzles me is that my coworkers have started replacing the gargoyles. That makes no sense."

"It does if they replace them in a different configuration," Mary said, reading over his shoulder again. "From the front of the cathedral, there are two points, one on each side of the entrance, so that the top point rises over the altar. If they turned that around, it apparently becomes the occult version of the pentagram. According to Aleister Crowley—and wow, I can't believe I'm using *him* as a source – that reverses the meaning. So the demons can escape with the use of that magical configuration."

Jon stared at the piece of paper with the crudely drawn pentagram on it. It made sense. The gargoyles were traditionally meant to protect the cathedral from evil. If that was true, then taking them down would leave the cathedral defenseless.

But what about the gargoyles that Hardy and his men were putting back? Suddenly, Jon was quite certain that these weren't the original gargoyles; that they weren't meant to ward off evil, but to invite it in.

"Do you suppose this pentagram design was on purpose?" Mary breathed. "That the builders knew this?"

"Since the cathedral was built by Freemasons, I would assume so," Jon said. "That's where the name Freemasons comes from—they were actually masons, and were the original builders of cathedrals. They were well versed in all arcane symbolism, and very little would escape their notice. Without a doubt, they felt they were protecting the cathedral by placing gargoyles on the ten points of this pentagram. It probably never occurred to them that anyone would reverse the symbol."

"So you're saying that not only is this cathedral haunted, but it is about to be invaded by demons," Mary said.

"I'd never say that," Jon said. "That would be crazy, wouldn't it?"

"What do we do?" she asked.

"We make sure they never complete the installation of the new gargoyles," he said.

He heard a scurrying sound behind him and turned with a shout. He would have felt foolish except that Mary had followed his example, even letting out a little screech of her own.

For just a second, a man and a woman were standing there. They were dressed in old-fashioned clothing, Victorian looking. They didn't look scary: indeed, the fright on their faces probably mirrored Jon and Mary's.

Then they were gone. There was nothing there.

"What was that?" Mary whispered.

"More ghosts," Jon said. He tried to say it lightly, but as soon as the words came out of his mouth, dread filled him, and he found himself reaching out for Mary at the same moment she was reaching for the comfort of his arms, and then they were face to face. He leaned down and kissed her.

It seemed to comfort her as much as it comforted him.

Chapter 25

I *wasn't going to do anything to her*, Father Michael thought as he hurried back to his office. *Mary surprised me, that's all.*

"Let he who is without sin," Father Michael muttered to himself.

He half expected to see the ghost of Father Gregory down in the catacombs. It seemed like just about everyone else had. One thing he knew: he wasn't like that disgusting pedophile, preying on his young charges. No, all his affairs had been with women and had been consensual. Sure, he'd broken his vows, but no one had been hurt. Besides, he'd long ago decided that it was the vows of chastity that were unnatural, not him.

Still, he couldn't shake the look of contempt in Jon's eyes; or worse, the fear in Mary's. They had misunderstood—he had merely been surprised. He wasn't a monster, not like Father Gregory, who had represented everything that was wrong about the way the church handled the abuse scandal. The lecherous bastard had been moved around, his crimes covered up, and ultimately, the consequences were never dealt with. "Let God deal with it" had been the prevailing feeling among the clergy.

Yes, I've broken my vows, Father Michael thought, feeling stronger with every step he took away from the unfortunate incident. *But there is a huge difference between breaking my vows and what Father Gregory did.* After all, he hadn't been planning to actually do anything to Mary.

"Are you so sure?" Father Michael asked himself aloud, then looked around to make sure no one was nearby. He let himself search his soul for a moment—an unusual experience for him. No, he'd been angry, but there had been no sexual threat involved. He was sure of it.

By the time he reached his office, he was feeling good about the arrangement. *Let her stay. If she's truly in danger, I am giving her sanctuary.*

There were two men standing outside his door, one on either side. They had the look of professional muscle—bodyguards or cops.

"Who are you?" he demanded.

They didn't answer. One of them reached over with his meaty hand, opened the door, and ushered Father Michael inside.

There were three more burly men inside, two of them young and on guard, the third older and sitting comfortably on the sofa on one side of the room. The cushions under the big man were pressed nearly to the floor; like most everything else in this old cathedral, the sofa was a castoff, a leftover. The man rose smoothly and extended his hand. He was dressed well, but his face was rough, and it looked as though his nose had been broken more than once. A front tooth was chipped, and one ear looked mangled. The man looked like he was only two steps up from the street.

"Father Michael? My name is Gino Pirelli," he said. "I'm looking for someone."

From the moment he first saw them, Father Michael knew these were the men Mary Patronis was running from. He composed himself, making his expression neutral. "I doubt I can help you," he said. "This cathedral is currently undergoing renovations. We have few parishioners."

"I understand," Pirelli said. "But your doors are still open. And I'm sure you have some unofficial visitors, here and there."

"Not if I can help it," Father Michael said, which was true enough.

"Her name is Mary Patronis," Pirelli continued, ignoring him. "She worked for me and has stolen some very important information."

"That's none of my business," Father Michael said. "And even if she came to me and confessed, I'd be compelled to protect her confidentiality."

"Ordinarily, I'd understand." Pirelli gave him a big smile. "I'm Catholic myself. But this isn't information that she had any right to. She stole it. Surely that makes a difference."

"It makes no difference, unless someone is in danger."

Gino Pirelli had kept a polite distance, but now he moved so close to Father Michael that the priest had the urge to back away. He held his ground, looking up with a forced smile into the man's now-glowering face.

"If I don't find her, someone's life may very well be in danger," Pirelli said.

The implication couldn't have been clearer. On the word "danger," the gangster—for that's what he was, Father Michael had no doubt—leaned in and nearly spit out the word.

Father Michael went around the man and reached for the phone on the desk. It was pulled abruptly from his hands as the gangster ripped the cord from the wall.

"I'm not leaving until you tell me where she is," Pirelli growled.

"I don't know where she is," Father Michael said. He'd always been a good liar, but even he was amazed by how calm his voice was.

The gangster also seemed surprised; then a sly grin came over his face. "You're taking this intrusion awfully well. Seems to me you should be more outraged. That is, unless you know why I'm here and are covering up."

"I am *completely* outraged," Father Michael sputtered. "This is the house of God. You will pay for this, on Earth and in…"

"Bullshit," the gangster interrupted. "I investigated you before I came here, Michael McCarthy. You're a fraud. You're a philanderer. Horny little bastard. And corrupt too, though they never caught you. You're exiled to this barren hulk because no one else will have you. This cathedral doesn't feel the slightest bit holy to me. In fact, it gives me the creeps. So quit all the posturing and tell me where Mary Patronis is."

Father Michael stood there with his mouth open. A day before, an hour before, if you had asked anyone who knew him whether he would stand up to a threat, no one, including Father Michael himself, would have answered yes.

But something unexpected happened at that moment; something that had probably always been there, but never put to the test.

The divine righteousness of Father Michael's youth returned in that instant, like a miracle bestowed from God. He'd always thought he'd be a martyr, dying in some hellhole tending to those less fortunate. He'd thought he spend his days on his knees, praying at the sound of bells, washing the feet of the poor.

Instead, he'd been nothing but a glorified accountant. The few times he'd been given the opportunity to minister, he'd failed completely, unable and unwilling to let go of his pride, to bend to those who were called "less fortunate"—but who, in real life, were miserable human beings who didn't appreciate his efforts.

Now, all of a sudden, he was confronted by a clear-cut test of his faith, and to his own great astonishment, he welcomed it.

"I have no idea what you're talki…"

Pirelli reached up with his huge right hand, wrapped his fingers around Father Michael's neck, and slammed his head onto the desk. A blast of light and sound pushed everything else out. All of Father Michael's holy righteousness disappeared. He couldn't even remember his name for a moment, or where he was.

"One more chance, *Mr. McCarthy.* Tell me where she is."

Father Michael began to form the words "She's in the catacombs," but something stopped him: not the glorious ecstasy of a martyr, but the simple reality of a young woman who was in danger.

"I'll pray for you," he said, as the gangster slammed his head against the desk a second time. He felt the edge bite into his forehead and then felt blood spurting down his face. The worn carpet rushed up to meet him, barely cushioning the blow from the ancient stone floor beneath. Then he was looking up from the floor at the disgusted expression on Gino Pirelli's face.

"Fuck," one of the bodyguards said. "He's smiling."

"Fan out," the gangster said. "She's here, or this self-righteous prick wouldn't be sacrificing himself."

The pain wasn't as bad as he'd thought it would be. The self-satisfaction Father Michael felt was far stronger, infusing his body with endorphins. Doing right felt good. It felt virtuous. Maybe he should have tried this sooner.

Forgive me, Father, for I have sinned.

129

The gangster's boot slammed into his midsection, and he felt the wind of a second kick heading toward his head wound, and then he felt nothing at all.

Chapter 26

The moment he realized he was moving, Dominic froze. *How did that happen?*

He tried moving his legs, his mouth, his eyes. Frozen, as ever. *Did I imagine it?*

"Try flapping your wings again," Pretty urged, thereby verifying that it hadn't been an illusion.

Dominic strained to move every part of his body, if only a fraction of an inch. Nothing.

"He was worried about the woman," Grotesque said to Pretty as if Dominic was a specimen they were examining. "Perhaps if we were to point out that she is still very much in danger?"

It's true, Dominic thought, the alarm returning. *Mary is still in danger. Why isn't that enough?*

Once again, he felt a fire burn through his body, which he recognized as a precursor to movement. Nevertheless, this time he remained motionless. He was a gargoyle, made of stone, cursed to remain immobile for eternity.

He must have broadcasting his thoughts, because Pretty immediately contradicted him. "That was not the curse you told us about, Dominic. The curse was 'Until you love someone more than you love yourself, you shall be damned to eternal silence.'"

Grotesque added, "Seems to me that you've met that requirement. Indeed, you moved only when you were more concerned about Mary than you were about yourself. I will repeat, sir, that Mary Patronis is still not safe."

"She is too good for me," Dominic said.

"Ah," Pretty mused. "So that's your problem. You still think that you can win her somehow. Forget it. That will never happen. It may be that she'll never know you exist, much less understand your longing for her. You must help her without any thought of reward, Dominic. Only then will you be free."

"But how?" Dominic cried. "What can I do?"

Grotesque and Pretty fell silent at that. In that silence, Dominic felt the deadness around him, the sleeping and benumbed gargoyles who had once protected the cathedral and were now removed from their duty.

"It cannot be a mere coincidence," Pretty said finally. "There must be *something*…"

Alastair suddenly appeared between them, followed by Margerie. "I believe I may have the answer to that. Mary Patronis is not the only human in danger."

"You found her?"

Margerie nodded. "She was in the archives, sleeping. Jon Williams joined her. Together they discovered what is really happening here."

"Explain," Grotesque bluntly demanded.

"First of all, you must understand that both Margerie and I have felt the presence of another ghost in the cathedral for a long time," Alastair said. "But we have never been able to find him. It was as if he was warded, protected by some greater power. We could not penetrate even the room with the other gargoyles in it. But neither Margerie nor I thought it was our problem to solve. We must beg your forgiveness for that oversight."

Margerie took up the story. "Alastair and I have been bickering over meaningless things for so long, we forgot—perhaps on purpose— that we are ghosts. We failed to recognize the danger until now."

"We understand that we are dead," Alastair said. "We know that we are serving penance for our sins, but that someday, God willing, we will move on. But we also remember that we once lived, that we were once human. We should have cared more about that, and tried harder to protect these holy premises."

"We have discovered this is the ghost of Father Gregory," Margerie said in a low voice. "I assume you remember him?"

Dominic could feel the shock of recognition coming from both Grotesque and Pretty. He himself remembered the name vaguely. A priest who had presided over the cathedral in the recent past? It was a fuzzy memory, coming from one of those times when he had been mostly asleep.

"I had hoped he was rotting in hell by now," Pretty said.

Margerie shook her head. "I believe he means to bring hell to us! Alastair and I intend to confront him, as soon as we can find him. But meanwhile, the cathedral is in danger."

"In what sort of danger?" Grotesque demanded. "Are you speaking of the danger to Mary Patronis and Jon Williams?"

"To them," Margerie agreed. "But to everything else in the cathedral and to everything beyond as well. I believe they are trying to open a gateway from the Darkness, that they mean to bring about the Apocalypse itself."

"Oh, is that all?" Grotesque laughed shakily. "I thought we were in trouble there for a moment."

"How do they mean to bring this…Apocalypse…about?" Pretty asked.

Alastair took a deep breath, a habit left over from when he'd been alive. "Perhaps we should start the way Jon Williams did, with the works of Aleister Crowley. You have heard of him?"

"I used to overhear the priests discussing him," Pretty said. "An evil man, I believe. Into witchcraft."

Alastair scowled. "He brings shame on our name: at least his is spelled differently. But it seems that he knew of what he spoke. Jon Williams discovered that if you draw lines between the places where the gargoyles have been removed, it represents a pentagram."

"Makes sense," Pretty said. "Pentagrams are meant to protect, as are the gargoyles. So someone is weakening the protections by weakening both."

"Worse," Margerie said. "Aleister Crowley maintained that turning the pentagram upside down reverses its effects. Instead of blocking evil, it invites evil in. The pentagram becomes a gateway."

"The other gargoyles," Grotesque said. "*That* is why they were created."

Alastair nodded. "And they are almost finished installing them. There is but one slot left unfilled." Both Alastair and Margerie turned to Dominic.

Dominic suddenly understood. A calmness came over him that wasn't anything like the petrified helplessness he usually felt. This lack of movement came from suddenly knowing what he was supposed to do.

He could move now, he understood that without even trying. He knew exactly where he was supposed to go.

"They mustn't complete the pentagram," he said.

Dominic raised his wings and flapped them once, and dust blew throughout the room, covering the other gargoyles. It seemed to him, for just a moment, that he felt some of the other gargoyles stir inside.

"Farewell, my friends," he said, lifting off the stone floor. He felt light, as if he was made of flesh and bone. Perhaps he was. Perhaps he had become fully alive. He didn't know and didn't much care.

He crashed through the stained-glass window, expecting the shards to cut into him, but he felt almost nothing, barely a tickle, and then he was airborne, flying high above the tree-lined street. The air flowed over him, and he could feel the currents and adjusted as if he'd been flying all his life.

He caught a strong updraft and drifted back over the cathedral. Below, he saw the new gargoyles staring up at him, stirring in their places as if they wanted to rise up and attack him.

Hardy and his men were wheeling a gargoyle across the roof toward the front of the cathedral. The crane was already erected, ready to be loaded and lowered. It was situated directly above the eastern side of the front entrance, the place where Dominic had spent the long years of his afterlife.

He flew down low over their heads, and the men shouted in alarm, letting go of the straps that held the big gargoyle on the cart. It swayed once or twice until Hardy reached out with a big hand and stabilized it. He stared into Dominic's eyes as if recognizing him.

Dominic swooped over the side of the balustrade and coasted down into the small niche above the elm tree. It seemed so small and isolated. As he settled into the spot, he marveled that he'd spent so much time in this one place. He looked out over the city, recognizing the old familiar landmarks.

He was home. No one was going to take his place without a fight.

"He can't do it alone," Pretty said. "The original gargoyles must help him."

"How are we supposed to do that?" Grotesque said, not hiding his surprise. "Unlike Dominic, we were never human. We have always been stone."

"But we have consciousness as well," Pretty said. "At least, most of us used to have consciousness. What was the purpose of that? That we sit century after century doing nothing?"

"Well...yeah," Grotesque said. "Pretty much that."

"That can't be all there is," Pretty insisted. "If the evil gargoyles can move, it must mean that the protective gargoyles were also meant to move when the time came. There must be a way to wake them up."

"Perhaps we should ask Father Michael," Margerie said.

"Oh, good idea," Grotesque scoffed. "Do you ghosts want to do it, or should Dominic fly over and ask him?"

Alastair looked to be deep in thought. Then he turned to Margerie and raised his eyebrows. She nodded back. "I think it's up to us," he said. "I believe Dominic will have his hands...his claws...full."

Pretty said, "There must be an activating prayer; *something*. I believe this is all fate, and that just as Dominic was meant to awaken at this time, so too are the rest of the gargoyles. Father Michael must know what to do, or all of this has been for nothing."

Grotesque shook his head. "Father Michael? I think we're in trouble."

"We have to try," Alastair said. "I can be convincing when I need to be. Maybe a little appearing and disappearing will convince him. We'll return." He nodded to Margerie, and they disappeared.

Grotesque and Pretty were quiet for a time after that. They could hear howling outside the windows and they knew Dominic was in a fight for his—and their—lives.

"We've got to help him!" Pretty cried suddenly, and to her and Grotesque's great surprise, a sound actually emerged from her mouth. It was a slight, strangled sound, but unmistakable.

"I think..." she said out loud, "...if I can speak, I can move." Then she was rising from the floor and spreading her small wings. She turned to Grotesque with wide eyes. "If I can do it, so can you!"

Grotesque frowned, and in frowning, realized that he could frown, and then it was as if every other part of his body had been unfrozen.

But whatever spirit allowed them to wake had also become noticeable to the demons, for one appeared at the broken window. It screamed a challenge, which Grotesque and Pretty both tried to answer. Grotesque flapped twice into the air and met the demon head-on in the middle of the room. Pretty screeched and attacked the demon's eyes.

The demon shook them off easily and swatted Pretty against the wall, and she slid down it and landed with a thud. Grotesque howled at that, picked himself up, and slammed into the larger beast, and for a moment it appeared he'd gained supremacy. Pretty shook herself, got up, and launched herself at the demon, but it was clear that they couldn't defeat this one opponent, much less the other demons outside attacking Dominic.

"Wake up!" Pretty screamed at her silent, unmoving brethren. "Wake up and do your duty!"

The frozen gargoyles didn't answer, any more than a rock would.

Alastair and Margerie popped into the middle of the fight, and both of them flinched and ducked to the floor, though the fighters' bodies went right through them. "Father Michael is on his way!" Alastair shouted.

"Go!" Pretty cried. "Help the humans. Help Mary and Jon!"

Chapter 27

"We have to stop them from installing the gargoyles," Jon said. He knew now why he'd been let go from his job early ("Full pay," Hardy had assured him.) If he'd stayed, he would have realized something was wrong, that the wrong gargoyles were being placed in the wrong spots.

How much have they done already? he wondered. The maintenance crew had always been lackadaisical, stretching out their jobs because there was so little to do. But if they put their minds to it, they could easily transport three or four gargoyles in a day. It had been almost three days since he'd last been at work, so they could be nearly finished by now.

"I can't believe Hardy would be a party to this," he said. But even as the words left his mouth, he doubted them. Hardy had seemed sympathetic to Jon's reaction to the hazing by the others, but he'd also allowed the bullying to happen. And there had always been a little undercurrent that Hardy hadn't really wanted him there, had only been acquiescing to the university's request because he'd had no choice. Now that Jon thought about it, his boss had seemed eager to have him go, early or not.

"How?" Mary asked.

"What?"

"How are you going to stop them?" she demanded. "How many are there? Do have a gun squirrelled away somewhere?"

Each and every member of the crew was bigger and stronger than Jon. He couldn't stop one of them, much less all of them. Jon shook his head. It didn't matter. He had to stop them, so he would stop them, and the how of it would have to come later.

He folded the paper with the pentagram on it and tucked it into his pocket, though he was pretty sure he wouldn't need it. He'd long ago memorized the positions of every gargoyle on the cathedral.

"Stay here," he said, and started for the door.

"No way, buddy," Mary exclaimed. "I'm coming with you!"

Jon hesitated. Truth was, he'd be glad to have her with him. She'd probably be safer in the archives, but…

"This is bigger than both of us," Mary said. "There is no safe place."

He nodded. They went into the airlock and opened the outer door.

Water started flowing over their feet in a steady trickle that didn't seem alarming at first until they realized that the water kept coming — and coming.

"Shit!" Mary cried out. She ran to the inner door and removed the duct tape from the lock. The door slammed shut with a firm finality.

The water had continued flowing and was now lapping at the bottom of the door.

"No going back now," she said grimly. "But at least the books are safe."

"Yeah, thank God for that," Jon said, not sure if he was being ironic or not.

Black water filled the corridor below them and was just reaching the first of the stairs. It had a strange odor, as if something alive and yet rotting was submerged beneath it. Jon cringed as he waded through the water, his hand out to help Mary. But it was he who slipped and she who kept him from going under headfirst. The water splashed over his knees as he tried to regain his balance. He felt as if something was going to reach out of the water and drag him down.

They reached the first step as the water was already starting to flow over the second step.

"Where's it coming from?" Jon asked.

"There's a pool of brackish water around the foundations," Mary answered. "I couldn't tell how deep it was."

139

"You've been there?" he marveled. Damn, he wished he'd thought of that.

Mary shuddered. "Father Gregory took me down there."

They hurried up the stairs as the water continued to rise quickly behind them. *By now the archives are underwater*, Jon thought. *I hope the airtight doors hold.*

They reached the top of the flight of stairs. If Jon remembered right, it was a straight shot from here to the offices in the levels below the nave of the cathedral. The water was flowing into the corridor behind them.

"How can it still be rising?" he muttered. "It doesn't seem possible!"

"A gateway to hell is opening," Mary said. "It has nothing to do with the possible. Everything from here on is the impossible. Get used to it, buster."

Jon couldn't help but laugh. He'd thought he was protecting her, but he was beginning to wonder if she wasn't the stronger one. She had accepted what was happening much quicker than he.

They were almost to Father Michael's office.

Is he part of this? Jon wondered. *Can he help? Do priests ever carry guns?*

Before they reached the last turn, two men came around the corner. They were both armed. The moment they saw Jon and Mary, they raised their weapons.

Jon found himself throwing up his hands in surrender, something he couldn't ever remember doing but which now seemed an appropriate response.

Mary was turning to run.

"Don't," the bigger of the two men said. "I *will* shoot you, Mary Patronis."

She stopped dead and turned slowly. "You can tell Mr. Pirelli I've already sent the information to the authorities," she said.

"So we've been told," the second man said. Both men were in ill-fitting suits, which seemed like costumes, mere disguises to hide their real jobs. "We're concerned that you might actually reach someone who will listen, however, so we need you to hand over the flash drive."

As they were speaking, the water continued to rise. The men seemed to notice it for the first time when it reached the tops of their shoes.

"What the hell?" one of them said, raising a foot.

"The flash drive is under a couple dozen feet of water by now," Mary said.

The two men looked at each other. One of them shrugged. "Then I guess we don't need you alive, do we?"

Both Jon and Mary turned to run. The water was up to their knees, and they had gone only a few feet before the first shot rang out. Jon tensed, expecting an explosion of pain. When it didn't come, he turned to Mary, expecting her to cry out instead. But she was looking back at him in wonder. There was a gouge on the wall beside them where the bullet had missed, though they had been only feet away from their attackers.

The water surged past them, knocking them both off their feet. The two thugs were trying to retreat. Something long and spiny rose above the tide, wrapping around one of the men. Shouting in fear, the second man shot at it, but the tentacle was flopping from side to side so quickly that the bullets missed. With each wave of the tentacle, the spikes ripped into the two men, smashing their faces into pulp, until their skulls shattered and there was nothing but a fountain of blood where their heads had been.

Suddenly, the water receded. Jon managed to get to his feet, holding tight to one of Mary's hands. They stood dripping, looking down in horror at the headless bodies.

Father Gregory appeared before them.

"They had no business interfering," he said, sounding sad. It was a phony sadness; Jon saw that now. Everything about Father Gregory seemed false now: the cheery, portly man, the kindly priest, the patient listener, the curious scholar. All bullshit.

"Why did you save us?" he asked.

"I have something else in mind for you two," Father Gregory said. He waved his hand invitingly up the now-dry corridor. They could hear the water below them, so it hadn't disappeared, but for now it wasn't rising.

Jon and Mary hesitated, and a scowl came over the heavyset priest's face. "Really, children, you have no choice." The water began sloshing up the hallway behind them again. "Unless you'd like to join those two."

Jon took Mary's hand, and together they followed the priest, but even as they entered the great cathedral, which should have been comforting, Jon knew that, if anything, the danger had increased.

Chapter 28

The water of Elk Lake was cool on his face, the waves rolling onto the shore from a passing boat. The sand was rough against his cheek. The sun was hot. God, how he had missed swimming in the Cascade Mountains, camping with his friends, fishing, hunting. It was so good to be back.

Why did I become a priest? Father Michael wondered. Only now, surrounded by nature, did he remember. *Because I loved God and I loved nature and I loved people.*

Not anymore. Going to the East Coast, entering the Jesuit order, ministering to the poor and the needy: all that had driven out his love of nature, of mankind, and finally even of God.

The sand was digging into his face, and it was beginning to hurt. He groaned and opened his eyes.

The water was still lapping at his cheeks, but instead of rough sand, it was the old shag carpet of his office that was rubbing up against him. The pain was sharp around his mouth, and he sat up, holding his hand to his swollen lips. Only then did it all come back to him.

The gangsters had demanded to know the whereabouts of Mary Patronis, and he'd held firm. And had gotten a beating for his virtue.

Still…it feels good. Maybe I should try doing the right thing more often…

He was dripping wet. The carpet was soaked, and he could see water stains on the sofa and chairs. *What the hell happened here?*

He managed to stagger to his feet, holding onto the back of the desk chair. He heard a rustle behind him, and he turned with a shout.

A couple was standing there, dressed in old-fashioned clothing. The man appeared to be older than the woman, and more prosperous. The woman was pretty enough, but was severe-looking, with her pulled-back hair and lack of makeup.

"Who are you?" he demanded.

"Alastair Hamilton," the man said, bowing.

The woman actually curtsied. "Margerie Marcotte." When she moved, it was as if he could see the curtains behind her. He squinted and it was as if they weren't there at all.

I've got a concussion, Father Michael thought. *I'm imagining things.*

"We are quite real, I assure you," Alastair said. "Though it is also true we aren't really here."

"Quiet, you," the woman ghost admonished her companion. "You're only confusing the poor man." She looked into Father Michael's eyes with an entreating expression. "We need your help, Father. The cathedral is in danger."

"Not just the cathedral," Alastair said. "If they succeed in entering here, nothing will keep them from the world outside."

"They?" Michael asked, though with a sinking heart, he thought he already knew. Something evil had been threatening this cathedral for a long time now, though he'd tried his best to ignore it. First had been the intrusion of Mary Patronis and Jon Williams into his ordered life, followed by the insolence of Hardy and his crew, then the specter of Father Gregory, then gangsters appearing out of nowhere, and now these…these ghosts of cathedrals past.

"I don't believe in ghosts," he said. *I don't believe in ghosts, or gargoyles who talk, or…God. And yet, the first two are undeniable true, and therefore, the third…?* Could he have been denying God all these years while God had kept faith with him?

The names of these two ghosts seemed familiar. When he'd first arrived and was still taking his duties seriously, he'd read up on the history of the cathedral.

"Alastair Hamilton…there was a man murdered in 1888 on the steps of this cathedral by that name," Father Michael said.

The ghost bowed. "At your service, sir."

"And Margerie Marcotte…a woman threw herself—and her unborn child—off the roof in 1901."

The female ghost curtsied again.

Father Michael shook his head, trying to clear it, which only redoubled the pain. "If I wasn't so wet and my head didn't hurt so much, I'd think I was still dreaming."

"You have never been as awake as you are now," Margerie said. "I've watched you, Father, while you tried to deny your belief. Yet it was always clear that in your heart, you knew God was watching."

Father Michael couldn't speak. He realized with some amazement that he was thinking of himself not as just Michael but as Father Michael for the first time in a long time. Why wasn't he more surprised? Margerie was right. He'd always seen the strange things happening in the corridors, had always felt the gargoyles watching him, noticed the presence of spectral figures in the hallways, heard the whispers at night. What was happening now was not so much a surprise as a confirmation.

"What do you need?" he asked.

Alastair quickly explained how the demon gargoyles were being positioned on an upside-down pentagram.

"So the devil may enter," Father Michael said after the ghost had completed the description.

"And all his minions," Margerie added.

"Hell itself," Alastair agreed. "If they open this gate, it will be the end of man on Earth."

"How do we stop them?" Father Michael asked.

"We have a friend," Margerie said. "His name is Dominic. He is a gargoyle, and he is alive. He is, at this moment, fighting the demons to keep them from completing the reversed pentagram."

"Dominic Carmelo," Father Michael intoned. "Murdered his wife and her lover in 1794. Was sentenced to become a gargoyle for all time."

"How do you know this?" Alastair asked. "We have never heard his full name."

"There is a book that I was given when I first came here. I read it, but I always thought it was fiction, the wild imaginings of bored monks. Supposedly, the guardian gargoyles were all men and women who were sentenced to purgatory for their crimes. There is a legend that someday they would come alive and protect us from a great evil."

"That day has come," Alastair said. "You must help us, Father Michael. Dominic is alone. He cannot hold them off for long. You must awaken the other guardian gargoyles to help him."

"Do you know how to do that?" Margerie asked.

Father Michael turned the chair away from the desk and crouched down to open the bottom drawer. It had become his junk drawer, where he threw things that he thought he might need, but which weren't important.

He lifted out piles of out-of-date warranties, old tax reports, expired receipts. At the very bottom was the small, scuffed book that Father Jonathan had given him. He turned immediately to the right page, as if every owner of the book had turned to that page, and more than once. Even he had read the activating prayer, fascinated by its very existence. This was the old Catholic Church, the medieval one, the magical, mystical, all-empowering one that had so intrigued Father Michael when he was younger.

"Show the way," he said, slapping the cover with the palm of his hand. "Let's do this thing."

"We will meet you in the room where the gargoyles are stored," Alastair said, blinking out of existence.

Margerie lingered. She had a sympathetic look on her face. "Be careful, Father. There are dangerous beings out there, mortal or immortal. And…" she grimaced. "You might not like what you see just outside your door."

Then she blinked away as well. Something about the way she said those last words filled Father Michael with foreboding. He began to open the door, but it got caught on the swollen carpet. He pulled it far enough to ease through and almost immediately slipped on the moisture in the hallway.

This puddle wasn't water, however. A blood pool covered the stone floor, moving slowly outward. The headless bodies of two gangsters lay between him and the stairway. He felt his stomach lurch, and he closed his eyes, afraid that he would see the bodiless heads staring at him. Then he opened his eyes, stepped carefully over the corpses, and began walking resolutely toward the cathedral above.

If I can just reach the sanctified grounds, he thought. *I'll know what to do.*

Chapter 29

"Spread out," Gino Pirelli commanded. "She's here or the priest wouldn't have tried so hard to tell us she wasn't." He turned to two of his men and pointed downward, and then motioned for the other two men to follow him up the stairs.

It was a huge cathedral, and most of it was open space. *There can't be too many places to hide*, Pirelli thought.

The light falling on his men's faces was a mixture of reds and greens and blues from the stained glass, but was bright enough that they could see into every shadow. The pews were narrow and low enough to the floor that no one could have hidden under them.

Pirelli had a vague memory of coming here as a child with his mom. She'd been so devout that she'd driven his dad away, and eventually Gino had tried to get away too. In the end, she still had enough of a hold on him that he kept her in luxury to the end of her life, and he pretended to still go to church. When she died, he was free to be who he really wanted to be. He still had a superstitious awe of priests—which was maybe why he'd been so hard on Father Michael. He didn't like being in superstitious awe of anything or anyone.

They quickly searched the nave, the choir, and the altar, then moved over to the transepts on either side. In the eastern transept, stairs led upward in a spiral, narrowing as they climbed higher. The first level was filled with small rooms with signs on the doors indicating that they'd once served as rooms for Sunday school classes or counseling. The next level was mostly storage rooms, which were mostly empty. On the third floor, the storage rooms were smaller and filled to the brim with discarded ancient machines or materials. Obviously, the priests had filled each one to capacity and then moved on to the next room.

On the highest level below the roof, the hallway was narrow and not well lit. There were only a few rooms here, most of them not much bigger than the average walk-in closet. Pirelli started to get that itching feeling between his shoulder blades that always warned him of danger and betrayal.

Well, not always, he reminded himself. *Mary Patronis caught me by surprise. I thought that bitch was well and truly bought.*

The first storage room was dark. There was no light switch. Pirelli pulled out his lighter and flicked it on. The light seemed to go about a foot in and then stop, as if there was a wall there. But he could sense the empty space, hear the echoes inside.

He hesitated at the door, then waved one of his men inside, handing him the lighter.

"Check it out," he said. "Every inch."

He turned away and nodded to the other man to follow. There was one more room on the floor. As soon as Pirelli opened the door, he felt a breeze. The room was long and narrow, with a broken window at the far end. A small curtain was flapping in the wind, and the light flickered. The floor was crowded with gargoyles, who, in the wavering light, appeared to be moving, turning their heads toward him, opening their mouths.

Pirelli blinked, and then stared down at the big gargoyle directly across from the doorway, which had a dumb look on his ugly mug. Pirelli laughed. Nothing here but mute stone.

He turned away and went back into the hallway. The man he'd left at the other storage room was leaning against the wall, breathing hard.

"What's wrong?" Pirelli asked.

"Nothin'," the man muttered. "Just gave me the creeps, is all. The place is empty."

"Where the *fuck* is she?" Pirelli demanded. He had a feeling Mary was near. There was one last place to check. He glanced upward. The ceiling was low, and he could hear footsteps above.

He hurried toward the stairs, making sure she wouldn't get by him. There was no one on the stairs, so he kept going up, followed by his two men. There was a crude door at the top, which was so ill-fitting that Pirelli could feel the wind blowing through. He pushed the door open and stepped out into the sunlight.

Five men in overalls were walking his way, hauling a cart with a huge gargoyle on it. They stopped in surprise at the sight of him, their eyes going to the gun in his hand. He put the gun in his pocket and widened his arms to show he was harmless, then motioned the men to come toward him.

"I'm looking for a woman," he said. "I'm told she spends a lot of time here. Just tell me where she is and I'll get out of your hair."

"A woman?" The largest of the men was a big, beefy older guy, with a black mustache and silver hair. He made even Pirelli feel small. He grinned. "I think you've come to the wrong place, buddy. Only us monks around here."

"Monks?"

"Well, we were once. What's the lady's name?"

"Mary Patronis."

"What do you want with her?"

Pirelli felt himself getting annoyed. "Does it matter? Just tell me if you've seen her or not."

"Oh, we've seen her. In fact, she's ours."

"Yours?" Pirelli tried to make sense of the conversation. The men didn't look frightened, despite Pirelli and his men's guns, and their gangster aspect that they made no effort to hide. "What do you mean, 'ours'?"

"Father Gregory needs her."

"I was told there was only one priest here," Pirelli said, finally realizing that the men were putting him on. One of them even seemed to be snickering. He pulled his gun back out. "We've already talked to Father Michael."

The workers laughed at that. "Father Michael don't know shit," one of them said, spitting.

Pirelli raised the gun, expecting the laughter to stop abruptly. Instead, the workers looked at each other and grinned.

"Can't have her, pal," the leader said. "Father Gregory needs her for the sacrifice."

Sacrifice? The word sent a chill down the gangster's spine. Behind him, one of his men stepped back, as if ready to run. Pirelli stopped him with a glance.

"Look," he said, modulating his voice as he would have to the don of another Family: a careful, calm voice addressing equals. "My name is Gino Pirelli. I have some pull with the Catholic authorities around here. I don't want to get you fellows in trouble. Mister…"

"Hardy," the foreman said. "Look, Mr. Pirelli. You seem like our kind of guy. You might do well in the near future, if you survive long enough. So we'll let you go. But you better scram right now. Shit's about to go down. Believe me, you don't want to be anywhere near here."

Pirelli tried one last time. "I don't care about what happens to Mary Patronis. I just need to talk to her for few moments, then you can do whatever you want with her. Understand?"

"I told you," the big man said. "She ain't talkin' to no one."

Pirelli couldn't believe it. He and his two men had the drop on these guys, guns pointed at them, and it had to be fucking obvious that they meant business. And yet these idiots were refusing a simple request.

Pirelli cocked his pistol. The sound seemed to echo in the open air of the roof. "I'm afraid I must insist."

A darkness passed overhead, like the momentary shadow of a bird. But it had to be the biggest bird to ever live, because the shadow continued to flow across the roof. Pirelli couldn't help but look up.

At first he thought it was a man paragliding. But the legs were too short, the wingspan too broad, and the head too huge. In the glare of the sunlight, it took Pirelli a few moments to get a good look at that face. His two followers were already screaming, and one of them was running for the door. Before he could reach it, another shadow dropped down onto the roof in front of him. This close, Pirelli realized the creatures were even bigger than he'd thought, towering over the humans.

Pirelli started firing without even thinking, even as the gargoyle swiped his escaping man across the throat. The claws cut deep. The man's head flopped back. Blood fountained onto the glowering face of the creature. The bullets bounced off his huge body, his massive chest and thick haunches.

The blood somehow brought the monster's features into focus. It had huge jaws, opened to reveal rows of sharp teeth and a long, forked tongue with a razor-sharp edge that flicked in the air, directing the flow of blood into his gaping maw. Its eyes were bulging and red, under heavy brows, malevolence beaming from them as if they were lit from inside.

The gargoyle that had flown over them was back, and it landed on the second gangster. Half of the man's body disappeared into its huge mouth, and then the man's bottom half was toppling onto the roof, his guts spilling out onto the stone. His gun slithered through the gore and landed at Pirelli's feet. He snatched up the weapon, turning, planning to take at least some of these bastards out before he died.

But it wasn't men he was facing. Instead, a row of monks were lined up in front of him, cowled figures, but where their faces should have been, slithering and twisting tentacles flowed toward Pirelli, and finally he screamed.

The tentacles were covered with sharp spikes that slashed across his face. He didn't feel anything at first, but heard his voice change tone as the throat that had directed the sound was opened up and the shout became a sloshing, choking noise.

He fell to the roof, feeling his blood flow out of his body, his eyes dimming.

Then Hardy was standing there again. "A fucking waste. We needed innocents to sacrifice, not the likes of you."

Pirelli felt a final, dim satisfaction that he'd somehow disappointed the beasts; then he was gone.

Chapter 30

Dominic heard the workmen yelling above him, as if they couldn't believe what they had just seen. Then there was silence. The fire within that had unfrozen him and that had given lift to his wings, lit by anger and concern for Mary, began to die down.

He'd have fought anything in those first few moments, but now he was given time to think. He'd seen the huge gargoyle in the cart. It was twice his size, and there were ten of them.

What chance do I have of fighting those monsters?

The streets below were empty except for a few humans scurrying in the distance, as if they could sense that something bad was going to happen. The air felt alive, a sensation that Dominic had never felt before and that—now that he was back in his old spot—he wished he could again experience in flight.

Where are they?

He sprang from his perch and instantly plummeted, falling toward the earth. He hit the upper branches of one of the elms and shattered them, raining leaves and twigs onto the street below. As the ground rose to meet him, one of his wings caught a stray updraft, and then the other wing, and he leveled and swooshed over the debris, sending it swirling in the air after him. He caught another, more powerful updraft that surged from the natural wind tunnel of the street below and rose swiftly.

Once again the exhilaration of flight filled him. How to position himself and when to flap his wings appeared to be instinctive. He needed to merely think about where he wanted to be, and his wings caught the air currents in such a way that he was directed there. But it wasn't just flight that so energized him, it was that he could move at all, that he was once again a free agent.

I could fly away from here, Dominic suddenly realized. *I could go somewhere far, far away.*

But what would happen to Mary?

He heard gunshots above him, and for a moment he faltered and began to plummet again. He quickly righted himself and caught an updraft, and this time he added a smooth, strong stroke of his wings. The stonewalls of the cathedral became a blur, and then he was surging over the balustrades, shooting far above the roof. He kept flying higher, just to see how far he could go and what it would feel like.

The wind pushed against him, and he began to drift away from the cathedral, but with a few strong downbeats of his wings, he steadied himself. He made a few small adjustments, letting the wind flow past him instead of catching or lifting him, and found a stable position far above the huge cathedral. The entire city opened up below him.

Dominic's view had been the same for two hundred years, and in that time, many things had changed. Buildings had burned down, or had been torn down to be replaced by more modern structures, and the roads had been paved, sidewalks added, trees planted and grown and died, power lines installed on posts and then later taken down and buried; cars had replaced horse-drawn carts, and once or twice, he'd even caught sight of airplanes in the distance.

But he'd never seen how *big* the city had grown, both outward and upward. He caught his first glimpse of skyscrapers, which he had understood existed but whose sheer scale he hadn't been able to truly envision. From this high up, the humans looked like insects, scurrying industriously about on inconsequential tasks, unaware that their existence was a mere speck of time to creatures like him. Just a few hundred yards away, a giant airliner rushed past him, sending him tumbling end over end. He caught himself and hurriedly flew back to his position of observing the cathedral.

So far, Dominic realized, his opponents didn't know he'd left his perch and that he was flying free. They no doubt thought he was trapped. Apparently they were in no hurry.

From up here, Dominic realized, he could see what they were up to and could react. He would have the space above them to maneuver in, and they wouldn't see him coming.

With any luck, the first skirmish would come as a surprise to them. He would swoop down upon them with all the power and speed that gravity could lend, and he would smash into them and break them apart, and they would see that it wasn't going to be so easy; that while he was alone, he was also determined.

He looked down, directly below him. There was a tableau of humans below, and though the two sides were unmoving, there was obviously a confrontation going on. The frozen scene was suddenly broken as one of the huge demons on the corners of the cathedral, one of the points of the pentagram, broke away from his perch. The demon's motion was so fluid, so natural, that Dominic suddenly felt clumsy.

I've been kidding myself, he thought. These creatures were never stone, never static. They had lived in the vast caverns below the cathedral, in the black abyss, doing their Masters' bidding. They knew how to hunt, to kill, to torture. It came naturally to them, and they had done it for who knew how long.

I'm a newborn, testing my wings for the first time, nearly plummeting to the ground as if thrown out of the nest.

A second gargoyle broke away from the other side of the cathedral, another point of the star. There were two groups of humans below. The larger group of five was made up of the workmen whom Dominic had watched moving about the cathedral for years, repairing and replacing things. The men facing them were dressed in suits and were brandishing weapons.

As these men started firing their guns, Dominic saw that he'd been wrong about the first group. They weren't human, but something else, no longer dressed in workmen's clothes but covered by cowled robes. Tentacles shot out of the cowls toward the humans, who were trying to get away.

155

The demons descended, and the humans didn't have a chance. They were slaughtered in moments. One man stood facing the robed creatures for one last defiant moment, and then he too was down.

The gargoyles landed near the robed creatures, and they appeared to be conferring. A few moments later, Father Gregory blinked into view. From a distance, the priest looked less than solid, as if he was wavering in midair. He was yelling so loudly that Dominic could almost, but not quite, make out the words. He was pointing toward the front of the cathedral, to where he no doubt thought Dominic was waiting, cowering.

Then the ghostly priest stood in front of the cart where the still-frozen demon was waiting. He began chanting loud, guttural, harsh words, which Dominic suspected that even if he could make out, he wouldn't understand.

The demon in the cart came alive, slowly unfurling its wings like a newly hatched bird, raising its head and shrieking at the heavens.

Dominic nearly fell from the sky with the fear that filled him. He'd been fatalistic, aware that he might meet his end in the coming confrontation, halfway hoping for it, grateful to be free in his last moments but unwilling to ever return to his unending purgatory.

But these creatures came from where he was no doubt going. There was no absolution for what he'd done; taking the lives of two people was not the type of thing that could be forgiven. Purgatory had been merely a way to extend his misery before he fell into the unending agony of hell.

I should be joining these demons, not fighting them.

But something deep inside, a dim memory of being mortal, kept him from taking that final step. Mary had awoken the human within him, along with the desire to be loved and to love. He would submit to his perdition, but he'd defy evil by doing one last good thing.

As if sensing his defiance, Father Gregory looked up at him. Everything became still for a moment. The wind seemed to die, but the sound of the humans screaming still lingered in his memory.

Come and talk, a voice said in his mind, and he realized it was Father Gregory. *I will call off the demons.*

For some reason, Dominic believed him, if only because he sensed the ghostly priest was supremely confident in his ultimate victory.

Dominic landed awkwardly.

"Why do you interfere, gargoyle?" Father Gregory asked.

Dominic didn't reply, but the priest seemed to sensed the answer anyway.

"I see now," he said. "You truly love her. You would give your own soul for her; thus you have broken the curse."

The priest shook his head ruefully. "I have to admit, Dominic, when I first met you, I was confused. It seemed like you might be one of us, because of the evil act for which you were condemned, and yet somehow you ended up in the storeroom with all the other dead and useless ones."

"Not all of us are dead," Dominic said. "Or useless," he added after a moment.

"Your friends are of little use. There is little you can do, Dominic. Join us, and you will live forever. You will be allowed freedom of movement. You will be one of the lords of this mortal realm."

"No," Dominic said.

"I see," Father Gregory said, shrugging. "Such a noble thing you're doing, Dominic, except...she doesn't even know you exist. She won't know that you sacrificed yourself for her. She won't thank you. It will be as if you never existed." The priest motioned to the demons, who stirred slowly.

Dominic surged into the air, flying higher and higher, while below, the demons and Father Gregory watched as if curious.

And then Dominic plunged toward them, screaming a fierce bellow he didn't know was within him, and it was the demons' turn to be surprised, to freeze in alarm. He slammed into the newborn demon, the one who was meant to take his place, and they both crashed onto the roof, shattering the stone slabs.

Dominic rose and began flying upward before the others could react. The demon he'd struck tried to rise, but one wing hung uselessly from its shoulder, and it stumbled and toppled over. It thrashed around, but seemed unable to get up.

The other two gargoyles flew after Dominic, but he'd gotten a head start, and he climbed with powerful strokes of his wings, exultant in his victory.

They won't be able to finish the pentagram!

Father Gregory was watching them, and now he turned toward one of the old gargoyles that lined the roof, the ones that had been installed many years after Dominic, the ones that looked like Grotesque and that were made of mere stone, without any spark of life.

The priest raised his arms, chanting, and the gargoyle began to transform. The injured demon stopped thrashing and grew still. At the same time, his replacement grew larger, his wings became wider, his jaws opened to reveal new rows of teeth, his legs thickened, and within moments, he was springing into the air, rising after his two fellow demons.

The priest looked up at Dominic with a grin. He transformed two more of the gargoyles into demons, as if to say, "No matter how many demons you defeat, there are legions more."

I can't defeat them, even if I beat them, Dominic thought. The demon priest could simply transfer their damned souls to another gargoyle. *What is the point of fighting?*

Once again, he looked out into the distance. A green forest still stood where he remembered it being as a living man—the grove of trees was bigger and taller now. A river ran between the forest and the city. In the distance, he could barely make out the ocean that was the reason this city existed.

All this would disappear if the demons won. There was no place for Dominic to hide. He searched his heart for the love he'd felt for Mary, and if in response, he felt her presence in the cathedral below, the imminent danger that surrounded her at this very moment, and without thinking, Dominic turned and dived toward the three demons following him, his claws outstretched, his jaws opened in screaming defiance.

Chapter 31

F ather Gregory led them to the center of the nave. There, the giant labyrinth embedded in the floor seemed to draw Mary, as if she was compelled to follow its turns, to reach the center, as if it would keep her and Jon safe. The church still felt holy to her at its heart, but the walls seemed to be closing in, as if the very stones had been corrupted. The sanctified ground was giving way to the relentless assault the forces of hell were summoning.

The priest gave the labyrinth a wide berth, as if he too sensed it would provide refuge. The church was empty, as far as Mary could see. All that was keeping them there was a ghost, she suddenly realized. The dark waters were below them, the creatures within it far away. She wondered, *Why are we letting him tell what us to do?*

"Let's get out of here," she said to Jon. She guessed from the wild look on his face that he'd been about to make the same suggestion.

He took her hand, and they started running for the front doors. Father Gregory flashed in front of them, his hands held out, but they ran through his image: a brief sensation of cold, and they were past.

With freedom mere feet away, Mary remembered Father Michael. She felt a moment of guilt about leaving the priest behind. But there was little she could do. If she and Jon stayed here, they would be trapped forever.

The huge doors towered over them. Jon already had his hands out to push on them when, from both sides of the transept, men appeared to block their way. They looked like monks, with long black robes, their faces hidden within the cowls. They stood side by side, and seemed to grow larger as Jon and Mary approached.

Jon pushed one of the men aside. "Keep going!" he shouted as three other monks surrounded him. Mary hesitated. The doors were only inches away. She could almost reach out and touch them. There was nothing between her and freedom.

The three monks didn't appear to be using their arms to restrain Jon, and yet he was being held by something, and he was twisting as if in agony. She saw his white face and open mouth, but no sound emerged from him.

Instead of running for the doors, she ran at one of Jon's attackers. Then she slid to a stop as she saw the swarming tentacles that were holding Jon, twisting his head to one side.

Another monk came up behind her, and she felt a sting between her shoulder blades. She fell to her knees on the hard stone floor, but there was no pain. In fact, she felt paralyzed from the neck down. As she struggled to hold her head up, the three creatures holding Jon let him go, and he crashed face first onto the floor, blood spurting from his nose and mouth. As Mary toppled to one side, she saw that Jon was still breathing, though he was unconscious. Two of the monks picked her up, and three of the others grabbed Jon, and they were carried to the altar and thrown on top of it, side by side.

Whatever had immobilized Mary was wearing off, and she managed to sit up, though she could barely maintain her balance. Jon remained completely out of it.

Father Gregory was standing behind the altar, grinning at her.

"Impressive," he said. "You shouldn't be able to move."

"Fuck you," she said. "Let us go, you bastard."

"You two aren't going anywhere," Father Gregory said. "Your souls are to be given to the Void, innocents sacrificed on the altar of Darkness."

"I told you," Mary said, "I'm no *fucking* innocent."

Father Gregory laughed. "A dirty word doesn't make you a sinner. Not in the real world; not below or above."

"What sins do you want?" Mary said. "Believe me, I've committed them. Greed? I worked for evil men because I wanted to keep my apartment. Envy? I wanted everything couldn't have. Anger? I've never been so angry as I am at this moment. Gluttony? Lust? I've given in to them both. Pride? I'm guilty of that above all. I'm a mess, can't you see that?"

"No, Mary, you're just human," Father Gregory said. "I never said you were without sin. And despite what my fellow priests might say, it takes more than that for the Darkness to consume you. I admit that I had my doubts that you were a suitable martyr, but when you finally turned on your criminal employers, that was good enough for me."

"Why now?" she asked. "Why not a hundred years ago? Why not when you first arrived? Why not, in fact, when you were still alive?"

"This cathedral has always been a reflection of the world around it," Father Gregory said. "The monks and their supernatural predilections—that was part of their times. But opposed to that was the true religious faith of the parishioners. Then, as time went on, the parishioners dwindled. The inner city surrounded the cathedral, and it became part of the general rot. And finally, a priest arrived who was as cynical as the world outside, a nonbeliever." He shrugged. "Maybe it was just that the Masters were ready. I don't know…the time has come, that's all."

Mary felt sensation tingling in her arms, and with a huge effort, she managed to move one foot slightly. *Wake up, Jon!* she cried out in her mind.

"Let Jon go," she said. "He's not part of this."

"Jon?" Father Gregory said. "Taking his soul may not be necessary, but it will please me nevertheless. He's been an annoyance from the start, interfering all the time, asking meddlesome questions, worst of all, getting the gargoyles all worked up. I should have killed him sooner. But…if you submit, Mary, if you do as I ask, I will let him go."

"What do you want?" Surreptitiously, she tightened her leg muscles. She sensed they would hold her up, that she could perhaps even run if she had too. But she couldn't leave Jon behind. *Keep Father Gregory talking*, she thought. *The ghost likes to talk.*

"The gargoyle Dominic is proving to be a problem," Father Gregory said. "But he seems to have a certain affection for you. Maybe if you call him, he will hear."

"Who?" Mary asked. The name seemed familiar, as if it was someone she knew well, and yet she couldn't remember ever meeting anyone by that name.

Father Gregory looked amused. "You don't even know his name? You've talked to him several times. He...it...is the gargoyle you cleaned first. Your touch has made him come alive. He's in love with you, didn't you know?"

"In love?"

Father Gregory laughed. "Ludicrous, I know. But here's the thing: Dominic the Lovelorn Gargoyle is in our way. I need you to call out to him, draw him away from where he is."

Mary knew that whatever he was offering was false, yet couldn't help but feel a small surge of hope. "If I call him, you'll let us go?"

"No," Father Gregory said. "I will let Jon go. You will have to stay, Mary. I need a sacrifice. But you have my word, if you do as I say, I'll let Jon go."

Chapter 32

Father Michael's foot had barely touched the second stair before the rolling wave of black water overtook him, grabbing at his feet, sucking him backward. He looked over his shoulder at the rushing water, swirling with creatures that skittered and danced, and he started running, taking two stairs at a time, out of breath by the first landing, but the tsunami kept coming, catching at him, turning the stone steps slippery and dangerous.

If he fell back into that maelstrom, he sensed, he would be stripped of his flesh in seconds. For though the creatures remained mostly beneath the surface, the parts that were exposed were tusks and hooks and suckers, glistening dark green flesh that undulated and hunted. He clutched the book high up on his chest, keeping it as far from the splashing water as he could.

He reached the main floor of the cathedral, and the water spilled out after him, but the vastness of the nave swallowed it long enough for Father Michael to reach the next flight of stairs. As he looked back, he saw a short, stout man in priest's robes at the altar. The water seemed to be avoiding him, though it was rising fast. Two people were sprawled on the altar, and though Father Michael couldn't be sure, it looked like it was Jon Williams and Mary Patronis.

Father Gregory was raising a knife over their bodies.

Father Michael opened his mouth to shout, but instead a bone-curdling scream came from above, and he closed his eyes and his mouth and clapped his hands to his ears. He opened his eyes as the first scream was followed by several more, lesser but no less threatening cries answering the first.

Father Gregory looked as if he was frozen in place. Then he slowly lowered the knife.

Father Michael couldn't move. There were shadowy shapes behind the altar, shapes he had seen many times in the old passages of the cathedral but that he had always denied, to himself and to others. In the book, it was written that a cabal of monks had once had ownership of this cathedral and had turned to the dark arts, creating the guardian gargoyles. But by doing so, they had corrupted themselves and the sanctity of the church, and brought about the very thing they had been trying to prevent.

The creatures in the robes—for they were not human anymore, Father Michael could tell even from a distance—began moving toward him, though it didn't appear they'd seen him. The swirling waters didn't impede them; they seemed float over the liquid, and they were rapidly approaching the staircase. Father Michael instantly understood that they were headed toward the same place he was.

The ghost of Alastair appeared on the step above Father Michael. "Hurry!" he cried. "The demons have discovered us!"

The ghost disappeared, then reappeared moments later, along with the ghost of Margerie, at Father Gregory's side. They both grabbed hold of the priest.

The dark water completely covered the floor of the cathedral and was starting to rise again. Father Michael shook himself and started running upward. He almost ran past the correct floor, but managed to turn at the last moment. He was out of breath, and his legs were wobbling from the exertion, but his fear was greater, and it seemed to him that he could hear the slithering sound of the monks and could feel their tentacles reaching out for him.

He threw open the doorway to the storage room. For a moment, he couldn't make sense of what he was seeing. His eyes finally resolved the shape of the gargoyles. One of the large gargoyles from the roof was locked talon to talon with something that superficially looked like a gargoyle but was something else. Unlike the gargoyle, which was the gray color of granite, the demon's flesh rippled and squirmed. It also bled, dark red blood that splattered about the room, falling on the heads and shoulders of still-frozen gargoyles.

Though bleeding, the demon seemed to have the upper hand, forcing the gargoyle backward toward the doorway—toward Father Michael.

A smaller gargoyle was also flying about the room, nipping at the demon's head and shoulders. Now it broke off its attack and flew directly at Father Michael, who flinched and threw up his arm. The book was taken from his hands, and the little gargoyle flopped to the floor and opened it.

"Yes! This is the book," the little gargoyle hissed. "Quickly, priest, read the Spell of Galvanization before it is too late. Grotesque can't hold off the demon for long!"

The creature held up the book, opened to the right page.

The gargoyle and the demon had been fighting in grim silence until that moment, but now an anguished cry emerged from the demon that nearly made the priest drop the book.

"Do it, Father!" the gargoyle named Grotesque shouted.

Father Michael looked down at the page. It was The Prayer to the Holy Angels, a prayer that he'd read before, but never spoken aloud. With a shaky voice, he began to recite:

"Bless the Lord, all you His angels, you who are mighty in strength, and do His will. Intercede for me at the throne of God, and by your unceasing watchfulness protect me from every danger of soul and body.

"Obtain for me the grace of final perseverance, so that after this life I may be admitted to your glorious company and may sing with you the praises of God for all eternity.

"O all you holy angels and archangels, thrones and dominions, principalities and powers and virtues of heaven, cherubim and seraphim, and especially you, my dear guardian angels, intercede for me and obtain for me the special favor I now ask: Give these guardian angels life!"

Before the last words were spoken, there was a rumbling sound and the floor began to shake. Father Michael nearly lost his grip on the book, but he shouted the last words, then closed the book and clutched it to his chest.

Father Michael visited this room many times. He liked the peace and quiet, the fact that no one would ever find him there. The gargoyles had always comforted him somehow. He'd always scoffed at them in public, but in private, they had become his secret friends. A layer of dust covered the statues, and in the clouded light of the dirty window, the room had felt abandoned, lifeless.

Just like me.

Now the dust filled the air. Through the cloud, the frozen sculptures began to move, slowly at first, as if waking from a long nap. There were low growls and mutters, and finally a screech from the small gargoyle.

"Wake up, you idiots!" the gargoyle cried. "Your time has come! Awake and guard your people!"

Chapter 33

"Why me?" Mary objected again. "I'm nothing special. I'm as flawed as anyone else."

"But you have a good heart," Father Gregory said, "and that's good enough. All that's really necessary to bring about the Apocalypse is the pentagram. The blood sacrifice just helps it along, that's all. You'll do. But even more importantly, that silly gargoyle is infatuated with you. He'll come if you call him."

Mary wanted to escape, but realized that it was hopeless. But if this priest was telling the truth, Jon might still live. All she had to do was call on a creature that wasn't real.

He's in love with me? she thought. *But what does that even mean?* He was a gargoyle, a mythical beast, and something to which she had no allegiance, whatever it might think.

And yet.

Why did it matter to Father Gregory? How could one gargoyle be so important?

She remembered the pentagram Jon had drawn, the conclusion that it was being inverted, turned upside down, meant for evil purposes. This gargoyle, this Dominic, was one of the guardians, she guessed. Somehow he was keeping the powers of darkness from completing their invasion.

"I won't call him," she said. The words came out before she realized she'd made the decision. "You're going to kill us no matter what I do.

And even if you don't kill us now, if we let this gate open, there will be no place to hide."

"Very wise of you," Father Gregory said. "I *am* going to kill both of you. All I really needed was for you to think of Dominic, and to be afraid. I assure you, he is well aware of the danger to you by now. Unless I miss my guess, he will not be able to resist coming to your rescue."

There was a rushing sound, as if the wind had broken through the stained-glass windows, and it took several moments for Mary to realize it was water, not wind, and that a wave was flowing through the cathedral, gathering strength, splashing up against the altar. The water was black, and snakelike creatures swirled and twisted in the fluid as if in agony while other shapes, more substantial yet harder for the eye to make out, jumped in and out of the waves. She could see teeth and claws and eyes, knowing eyes watching impatiently.

"I see that we had best get started," Father Gregory said. "My Masters are impatient. They've been waiting for millennia." He pulled a long knife from his robes and raised it over his head.

Then, above the roaring waters, came a cry that made Mary despair. Until that moment, she'd been frightened and angry, but there had still been fight in her. But that cry was so violent, so wicked, that she understood that something truly evil was about to be loosed upon the world.

To her surprise, Father Gregory's reaction was even more pronounced. His head jerked upward, and it was as if his eyes moved of their own accord, as if he could see through the stone pillars. He grunted something in a language Mary couldn't understand, harsh and painful to the ears.

Father Gregory looked down at Mary as if furious at her, but she could see from his eyes that his thoughts were elsewhere. Then he focused on her with a grimace.

"I must go," he said. "I wish I could have completed the sacrifice myself. I would have enjoyed that. But it doesn't matter. You can't move, and the dark waters will soon be upon you. The demons of the dark waters will consume you. Just as well. They'll be hungry."

He started to fade away, but then suddenly reappeared. On either side of him were two other ghosts, each of whom had grabbed an arm. They were becoming more solid with every second. The male ghost was dressed in a dark suit with an old-fashioned cut. His tie was askew, as if he'd been in a rush tying it, and his gray hair was tousled. The woman was younger and smaller, but she had a wiry strength that appeared to be enough to hold the fat Father Gregory in place.

"You aren't going anywhere, Fath..." she faltered, stumbling over the title, then continued, "...Gregory."

Chapter 34

Dominic dove into the three demons, who at the last moment tried to split apart. The demon in the center, the one Dominic recognized as his replacement at his point of the pentagram, didn't get out of the way fast enough. Dominic crashed into it, and it slammed against the stone balustrade. Its spine bent in an unnatural way and then broke completely, and it flopped forward. Only the top half of its body could move. Dominic quickly loomed over it, slashing downward again and again until the monster wasn't moving at all anymore.

Father Gregory wasn't on the roof and wasn't there to replace it. Dominic sensed that the fight for the soul of the cathedral wasn't taking place only on the roof, and that Father Gregory was busy elsewhere.

The surviving demons attacked him from both sides, and once again Dominic tried to gain height on them, but they understood what he was doing now, and they quickly overtook him, clawing at his legs, nearly reaching his wings. Dominic realized that if his wings were injured, the battle was over: they need not finish him; they could safely ignore him and fly to their respective points on the pentagram.

Already Dominic could feel the evil invading below, filling the cathedral, but these creatures were merely forerunners, the overflow from the place beneath. The true denizens of the underworld were only now slouching upward, waiting for the gate to be opened all the way.

Dominic abruptly changed direction again, diving downward, weaving between the high towers and buttresses, keeping just out of reach of the demons. His shoulder slammed into one of the buttresses as he miscalculated his speed, and he caromed into the open air beyond the cathedral. The demons didn't follow, but stopped short as if blocked by something.

They are alive, Dominic thought. *But they are not yet free.*

As long as the inverted pentagram was incomplete, they could not leave the boundaries of the cathedral, he realized.

Free of their attacks, Dominic circled the cathedral, looking for a way to carry on the fight. They mustn't complete the pentagram, above all. He'd gotten lucky, catching them by surprise, killing two of them. But no matter how many he killed, Father Gregory could simply summon more.

As if in answer to his thought, the two surviving demons were joined by those who had already taken their place in the pentagram. They swirled about inside the boundaries of the pentagram as if waiting for Dominic to challenge them.

Then, one by one, they disappeared from view. As Dominic circled the cathedral, he saw that they were dropping back into place. As the last three demons faced him, he realized it would take but one of them to take his place and the pentagram would be complete.

He flew to the front of the cathedral, to the perch that had been his home for two centuries. With cries that stabbed out into the city, the remaining demons raced him to the spot. If not for the wind behind him, they would have easily beaten him there. As it was, he slammed into the niche mere moments ahead of the others. The wall splintered where he struck it, and for a moment he was stunned.

A sharp pain carved down his back, and he turned just in time to block his enemy's next slash, what would have been a killing blow. The three demons were trying to hover before him, but there wasn't enough room for more than one at a time to face him, nor could they maintain their positions in midair for long. Neither gargoyles nor demons were designed to hover in one place. They weren't hummingbirds.

With a cry of frustration, two of the demons dived downward, gaining speed before shooting upward again. The remaining demon tried to grab hold of the side of the cathedral, but one on one, Dominic felt secure enough to leave his protected corner and drive outward with his legs, pushing the demon away. It fell backward, desperately trying

171

to catch the wind in its wings, but it crashed into the branches of the elm below and then down to the concrete, where it thrashed about on its back but could not right itself.

Pieces of shattered stone surrounded Dominic, and he picked up the biggest chunk and dropped it down on the demon. By luck, it landed squarely on the creature's head, obliterating it.

The other two demons returned, and they took turns diving down upon Dominic's hidey-hole, slashing with their long claws. All Dominic could do to protect himself was to raise his own arms and claws. Deep wounds cut into his flesh until strips of it hung from the bones, and blood spattered the surface of his perch. He howled in agony, though he knew it would give his enemy hope.

For decades, he had felt nothing. Not the harshest sleet blown by the strongest winds had affected his stone surface. He'd forgotten the pain of being alive, of nerves exposed to injury.

But he held his position. They couldn't get an angle on him. He began to hope that he could hold them off indefinitely.

The demons broke off their attack. They circled above the cathedral, flying higher and higher, until they were mere specks to Dominic's eyes. Then one of the specks dove straight down, its wings furled, its head pointed downward, like a missile, and as it plummeted toward him, Dominic realized that the creature was heading straight toward him. It was suicide, but it would also be suicide for Dominic to be in its path.

The other demon was also falling, but at a controlled speed. It would arrive perhaps only moments after the first demon, but would be able to hold its position.

Dominic jumped from his perch at the last second, falling as the loud crash of the demon landing in his spot shook the air behind him. He looked over his shoulder as he tried to catch the air beneath his wings. His claws scratched against the concrete of the sidewalk as he caught the wind at the last second and veered upward. There was little left of the attacking demon but a mass of splintered bone and flesh.

But the second demon was already settling into the spot.

With a cry of despair, Dominic dove at the intruder, but now the situation was reversed and Dominic was the one frustrated by the narrow space and angle of attack. The demon was securely entrenched.

The inverted pentagram was complete. The skies about the cathedral grew dark and sound was muted; it was as if everything had slowed down. Dominic felt his thoughts slow, and his sense of self, so strong and defiant just moments before, became hushed and deadened.

It was at that moment he felt Mary's cry of pain.

Chapter 35

The awakened gargoyles filled the room with the frenzied beating of their wings. Father Michael backed away until his back hit the closed door. He couldn't breathe, and when he did gasp in some air, it was less air than dust, and yet he didn't cough, he just took it in, frozen in place as if replacing the now-mobile gargoyles with his own rigidity.

The demon was now trying to get away, but Grotesque held it in place. First one gargoyle, then another attacked the demon, until it broke apart, its wings flayed and broken, its horns snapped off, its fangs biting down uselessly on hard stone, splintering. It cried out, its voice seeming the swirl the dust, and then it was still. The pieces of the creature lay scattered on the floor.

The gargoyles swirled about the room, faster and faster, like moths caught between windowpanes, their wings smashing against the walls, barely missing Father Michael in their frenzy. Then, one by one, the gargoyles shot out of the window and disappeared, until only the two that Father Michael had found mobile were left.

The bigger gargoyle, as beaten up as he was, made as if to follow his brethren, but the smaller gargoyle cried out, "Wait, Grotesque! Mary and Jon are in danger. Dominic would want us to help them."

Father Michael fell to his knees, struggling for breath, feeling as though the dust had congealed in his throat. His eyes were so gritty that he could neither open them nor close them completely. He wiped his forearm across them, which only made it worse.

"They're at the altar," Father Michael gasped. "Father...no, he's no priest...the *devil* Gregory is with them. I think...I think he means to sacrifice them."

The two gargoyles didn't answer. They simply flew toward the doorway, and Father Michael opened the door and ducked out of the way. Then the room was empty and quiet, and Father Michael decided he wasn't moving again until it was all over. He collapsed on the stone floor, as if his muscles had lost all shape and his bones had liquefied.

Maybe I'm a priest after all, he thought. *But even God can only ask so much of me.*

But even as he thought it, he knew he wasn't finished.

Dominic felt Mary's pain and dismay as if it was his own. He flew toward the broken window through which he had so recently escaped, but as he approached, it was as if the cathedral was pushing him back. No matter how hard he beat his wings, he couldn't get closer than a few feet.

Mary had brought him to life again, made him remember, made him care. She didn't know he existed, not really, and yet it didn't matter. The love he felt for her was so strong that he would have willingly left his place on the cathedral to save her, even if it spelled the doom of mankind.

Fortunately, perhaps, the cathedral had other ideas. Whether it was the darkness within that was keeping him out, or whether it was what was left of the sanctified grounds, he didn't know.

He cried out in frustration, sounding more like a demon than a gargoyle. He flew upward, higher and higher, looking down at the blackness that surrounded the cathedral. The building itself had a red-tinged glow, as if it was burning from inside.

Dominic could see the reverse pentagram as if it had been inscribed, his eyes drawn to the five points and five indices, all occupied by creatures bigger and stronger than he was.

I only have to defeat one, he thought. *If I can dislodge one of them, the pentagram will be broken.*

Father Gregory had created more demons than he needed. The surplus creatures were flying in tight circles around Dominic's point on the star, guarding it.

There was one last thing he could do. He could follow the example of the demon that had driven him from his spot. He could sacrifice himself to break the hex. They wouldn't be able to stop him.

And afterwards? They'll just replace the demon I destroy. They'll replace every demon I destroy.

The black void surrounding the cathedral was reaching up to him with long, spectral fingers. He felt sluggish, barely able to flap his wings enough to stay aloft. Despair filled him. There was nothing he could do. He was alone against ten stronger opponents. He couldn't even help Mary in her time of need.

He would break the pentagram, he decided, if only to forestall the inevitable for a few moments. It was all he could do.

But his attack didn't have to be where they expected him. If he attacked the point farthest away from the one where the demons were waiting and dislodged the one there, it would take them that much longer to replace it. It might only be a few moments longer, but Dominic knew that he wasn't completely alone. Father Michael and Mary and Jon were all inside the cathedral. Perhaps, by breaking the pentagram, he would give them a few moments of respite, enough time to make a difference.

He prepared himself. He didn't know what would happen when this body he inhabited was destroyed. Would he become a ghost, like Alastair and Margerie? Would he simply cease to exist? Or would he go to the hell he deserved, the one he was so ironically fighting against now?

As sluggish and tired as he felt, he was still alive, he was still moving of his own free will. It was hard for him to believe that he'd ever endured the decades unable to speak, to move, barely able to maintain his consciousness. Maybe it wasn't so much that he'd endured it; after all, he'd had no choice. But now he had a choice, and he knew he never wanted to go back to that.

He started climbing. He would make sure that he came in at such a speed that no one and nothing could stop him. A few last moments of exhilarating speed, the rush of air, the sight of the city below, and a final sacrifice.

Whatever God had in store for him, he'd soon find out.

Father Gregory stiffened under Alastair's touch. He almost broke free of Margerie on the other side, but she clamped down, her ghostly fingers digging into ghostly clothing, not letting him go.

The demon priest tried to shimmer away, but couldn't as long as the two other ghosts holding him also held to their corporeal forms.

"You're not going anywhere, Fath..." Alastair's voice faltered. Like Margerie, he couldn't complete the honorific. "...Gregory," he finished.

"Help me!" Gregory cried, and the monks moved toward them. Alastair and Margerie blinked out of sight, taking their captive with them. They hadn't conferred with each other, but the long decades in each other's company had made each aware of the other's thoughts and actions. Their bickering had long ago become affectionate, their annoyance feigned. They knew each other's mind as well as their own. Together, they decided to take their captive to the room where Dominic had been stored.

Father Michael was lying in the doorway as if asleep. But he sat up immediately at the sight of them.

"This cathedral is infested with ghosts," Alastair said. "It is time you did your duty and banished them."

Alastair looked toward Margerie, who nodded.

"But if I do that, won't you...?" Father Michael began.

"Ghosts don't belong here, Father," Margerie said. "They belong in heaven…or hell, as the case may be."

Father Michael got to his feet. He was still clutching the Book of Protection Prayers.

"Do you have something handy in that book?" Alastair asked. "Something that will banish all ghosts?"

The priest leafed through the book as if at a loss, as if trying to remember its contents. Then he stopped abruptly and an expression of resolve came over his face. He looked toward them and nodded.

"Then you better get to it," Alastair said. "Bad enough that demons are invading."

Margerie added, "You don't need ghosts to add to your troubles."

Father Michael looked down, studying the page. Then he glanced upward again, hesitantly. "Are you certain?"

"It is time," Alastair said.

"We will face our Maker," Margerie said. "Whoever He…or She…or It…is. And somehow, I think Gregory's Maker won't be too happy with him."

Father Michael raised the book and started chanting in a low voice.

Alastair had thought he was ready, but now, as the first words washed over him, he felt the same reluctance that had kept him on this mortal plane for so long. He looked beseechingly at Margerie. She smiled at him, and he felt strengthened by her courage and resoluteness.

He raised his chin and faced the end.

"I humbly ask that God, Father, Son, and Holy Spirit, descend upon me. Please purify me, Lord, mold me, fill me with Yourself, use me. Banish all the forces of evil from me, destroy them, vanquish them, so that I can be healthy and do good deeds. Banish from me all spells, black magic, diabolic infestations, oppressions, possessions; all that is evil, including moral, spiritual, diabolical ailments.

"Burn all these evils in hell, that they may never again touch me or any other creature in the entire world. I command and bid all the powers who molest me to leave me forever, and to be consigned into everlasting hell, where they will be bound forever.

"In the name of the Father and the Son and the Holy Spirit, amen."

Father Michael's voice had grown stronger as he spoke, as if he realized that the prayer was working.

Alastair felt himself letting go, spiritually, physically; mentally leaving his old concerns behind, his grudges, his rage, his pain. Margerie had a blissful smile on her face.

Even the look of horror on Father Gregory's face couldn't detract from the rightness of it.

As Father Michael performed the sign of the cross, Alastair realized that this was not an ending, but a beginning. And then light washed over him, and he understood everything: why he'd stayed, and why now he must go.

He felt one last sensation. The hand clutching Father Gregory burned for a moment, and he saw a black flame erupting in the space between him and Margerie, a void caught for a moment amid the glowing light. The demon between them returned to the fire, and Alastair took one last look at earthly realms, and saw the wonder on Father Michael's face.

And then Alastair Hamilton let the light of God envelop him.

Chapter 36

"Wake up, Jon!"

The woman's voice came as if from far away. Someone was tugging on Jon's arm. His feet felt as if they were immersed in a pool and tiny fish were nibbling on his toes. There was a sharp pain in his soles, and in his nightmare, those tiny fish turned into flesh-eating monsters.

He woke with a cry. Mary was looking down at him. He could make no sense of where he was. His body felt wrong, as if it was in two different places. He could feel the pain in his feet, but he couldn't move them.

He realized that Mary wasn't just shaking him, she was holding him up. He was on a flat surface with his legs hanging over the side, and he was being pulled off by something just out of sight. Something with sharp teeth that was penetrating the numbness of his lower body. Yet he barely had the strength in his arms to prop himself up.

He pulled himself painfully to a sitting position and looked down. Water was splashing up against the altar, and within that dark water were creatures churning in and out of sight, many of them massing around his submerged feet. There was a bright red color to the water, and to his horror, he understood that it was his blood.

Jon pressed his palms onto the slick surface of the altar, slipping several times before he was able to pull himself up an inch. Mary was trying as best she could to help him, and between the two of them, they managed to draw his feet up out of the water.

It wasn't as bad as his imagination had come up with. His feet were cut and bleeding, but nothing was missing. He sat cross-legged on the altar and looked around.

He and Mary were perched atop the altar, and surrounding them on all sides was the dark water, which appeared to be rapidly rising. He shook his head, trying to make sense of it. It was as if his brain was a lump of inanimate matter without a spark of thought.

Then it all came back to him. He looked around wildly. "Where's Father Gregory?"

"He's gone," Mary said. "I think...maybe for good."

"What about his creatures?" Jon asked.

As if in answer, cowled figures emerged from the shadows, rushing toward the altar.

The monks moved swiftly, floating over the water. Jon saw the wide tentacles beneath the robes swirling forward. Then the creatures surrounded them, and Jon's heart fell. Feeling was returning to his legs slowly, but he sensed that he couldn't stand upright. Mary appeared to be in slightly better shape, but the largest of the creatures was twice her size.

That figure came forward, throwing back his hood.

Jon tried to make sense of what he was seeing. It looked like his old boss, Hardy: at least, he had the same shape, and the wicked smile seemed familiar. But that face! It was bifurcated down the middle, and where the nose would have been was a dark red, fleshy fold with tentacles emerging from it, thrashing about as if they had their own motive power. The eyes were huge, with elongated red pupils. More tentacles, larger and slower moving, were attached to the top and back of the head. Large sucker-filled tentacles emerged from where the arms should have been.

Hardy's mouth was the same, but filled with sharp black teeth. Yet despite the alienness of this Hardy, Jon could somehow read his body language and expression.

"I'm sorry it has come to this, Jon," Hardy said. It was a human voice, just barely. If Jon hadn't already been used to his foreman's garbled tones, he probably wouldn't have understood him at all. "You should have left when you had a chance."

181

"Would it have mattered?"

"Not a bit, son. We would have got to you…to all you mortals…in the end. But you might have enjoyed a few days of freedom."

"Then I'm glad I have chance to tell you to fuck off to your obscene face," Jon said.

"That's my boy!" Hardy said, and the tentacles made a slithering noise that sounded like laughter. "You've finally learned the proper spirit. Tell the bastards to fuck off, I always say."

Hardy turned to the other monks, who had held back. "What do you say, boys?"

The creatures seemed to be trying to answer, but all that came out was slithering, sloshing, gnashing sounds.

Hardy turned back with an apologetic slant to his mouth. "You have to forgive them. They never much liked pretending to be human, whereas I always kind of enjoyed it. You know…as long as I knew it would come to an end. Speaking of which, I'm afraid we can't let you leave the altar. I don't think the Masters much care how you are sacrificed, so if I have to, I'll do the job. But I'd just as soon let our new friends finish it."

The water was continuing to rise. Mary held out her arms, and Jon embraced her. He closed his eyes, waiting for the first waves to splash against them.

Just as he felt the first surge of water against his legs, it suddenly receded. At the same time, there was a roaring sound, as if a gigantic wave was nearing a rocky shore, and Jon opened his eyes to see a huge mound rising up in the center of the cathedral, sucking up the black water around it, congregating the creatures within.

The pyramid of wriggling, seething creatures rose higher and higher. Clawed, horned, fanged things skittered about the surface, blood red and yellow puss-like gelatinous creatures holding the whole thing together with trailing tendrils of spines and suckers. The creature seemed to be molding all the life within it, arms sprouting from both sides trailing down to long claws, huge leg stumps developing in the water, and a blockish, eyeless head forming.

The creature moved slowly, but the parts of it moved in a constant frenetic motion, so overwhelming to the senses that Jon was forced to turn away. He could see the overall shape of the thing and sensed it coming alive, as if inhabited by a distant consciousness. The giant head moved ponderously, with its rippling, squirming surface, in the direction of the altar.

The colossus stepped forward, shaking the cathedral, shattering the stained-glass windows above. No light came through those windows, only a cloudy, inky darkness. Jon turned to Mary, and she put her face into the crook of his neck and held on tightly.

Its next step shattered the stone floor in front of the altar, and Jon and Mary nearly slipped off onto the now-slimy floor. A giant hand reached out for them.

Jon stood up, facing the seething hand, and shouted at the top of his voice, as if that would stop it. Mary stood up next to him and added her voice, yelling her defiance.

The creature's fingers wrapped around them and started to squeeze.

Dominic folded his wings and dove.

Below, gargoyles erupted out of the broken window at the side of the cathedral, flying about frantically, as if not quite certain what to do. One of the larger gargoyles sighted the pair of demons circling and cried out. It charged the demons, and moments later, several other gargoyles followed.

It wasn't just the ten gargoyles that had been removed from the pentagram, Dominic saw. It was every gargoyle in the storeroom, dozens upon dozens of them. The rows of gargoyles on the roof began to stir as well; slowly at first, and then with a growing agitation.

Somehow, they were being called into action. Somehow, they instinctively understood the demons to be enemies.

The gargoyles reached the first demons, and in the flurry that followed, pieces of stone and flesh flew through the air, but when it was over, the demons still flew and the gargoyles were shattered, falling. More gargoyles came, and again the demons fought them off. They were bigger, stronger.

But they were also of flesh. The stone gargoyles slammed into them, again and again, and the demons slowed, unable to respond to every blow.

Dominic leveled out his dive and began circling, watching the battle below. The clouds parted over his head, and bright sunlight washed over him. His numbness and dread lifted, and his strength returned. The light shot downward like spears from heaven and penetrated the darkness surrounding the cathedral.

The gargoyles were milling about, but didn't seem to know what to do. Dominic flew down until he was in their midst. They appeared to recognize him and circled him, crying out.

Dominic waited until he was surrounded, then flew to the first point of the pentagram. A demon that waited there rose up on bulky legs, wings outstretched, jaws issuing a howl of defiance. Dominic slashed at the creature, and then he was pushed aside as the other gargoyles rushed to follow his example.

He circled away and watched as gargoyle after gargoyle attacked the demon, to be crushed and broken, until at last, two of them took the demon on either side and thrust him out of his perch. Once the creature was exposed, the other gargoyles fell upon it, and through the shrieks and thuds, the demon was driven away. A gargoyle that Dominic recognized as one of his companions from the storeroom—who had never shown any sign of life before—took his place on the point.

Dominic flew to the next point in the star and again took the first swipe at the encroaching demon, and again the other gargoyles gathered after him, eager to do battle. The demon fought back with a furiousness that seemed unconquerable, but the gargoyles were equally determined. One by one, the demons fell, each replaced by the apposite gargoyle.

The darkness shredded, points of light tearing into it, the glow spreading, weakening the demons and lending strength to the protectors. The cathedral itself remained dark, its red glow undiminished. Dominic sensed that the pentagram would have to be fully reclaimed before the enemy within was defeated.

But as Dominic approached his own point in the pentagram, he realized his allies were dwindling rapidly. He let the others do the fighting, sensing that the last desperate battle would be his alone.

He left the last of his followers to attack the second-to-last point of the star and flew onward to his own roost. He hovered there. The demon in it glared back, its rage and menace undiminished by the defeat of its evil companions.

Dominic closed in, reaching out with his claws, his wings spread out behind him. There would be no retreat. Either he or the demon would occupy this spot, and with possession of this spot came the future of the cathedral and of the humans within—of Jon and Mary and Father Michael, and of humanity itself.

It all came down to this nexus, a single point on a star.

The demon was bigger than Dominic, able to dart downward with its jaws and rip into Dominic's shoulder, which began to shatter under the force. Dominic wrapped his wings around the demon and hung on, and then began to squeeze.

It was as if the very structure of the cathedral added to his grasp, as if every stone of its foundations lent him strength. The demon squirmed under the pressure and almost broke free, but Dominic bit down on the demon's wings, snapping them off one by one. The demon pushed outward, as if trying to get away, but Dominic pushed toward the stonewalls, as if trying to meld with them, and it felt as though the rock reached out to greet him. The demon was squealing now, a diminished sound, as if it knew it was defeated.

The sunlight grew around them, as if it had finally penetrated to the ground below and was bouncing back upward with ever more power. The light gave Dominic further hope and strength, and he felt the demon's flesh giving way, turning soft and liquid, until only the creature's head remained, its gaping mouth still making frantic sounds.

And then it was still.

Dominic was bathed in sunlight. The broken stone about his shoulder and wings knit back together, and he pushed off from his perch to let the shattered remains of the demon fall to the pavement below. Dominic flew upward, and the wind seemed to be directed at him alone, and he gained height without even trying, higher and higher until he could see the entire city, and directly below, the cathedral. It looked unbroken, shimmering in the sun, and Dominic could see the points of the star, the protective pentagram restored, all but one point.

He dove downward, swooped over his fellow gargoyles, who roared their approbation, until he was once again at the front of the cathedral. He slowly lowered himself into his perch and settled in.

Then, with a sound that was almost human in its triumph, he shouted out to the heavens.

The hand that closed about Jon and Mary was made of smaller hands and tentacles that bit into their flesh. Mary cried out in pain, and Jon tried to insert his body between her and the giant, but they were surrounded on every side.

And then, from a distance, they heard a triumphant shout. It was a human-sized shout, alien in its commonplaceness, but it seemed to shake the giant to its core. It heaved suddenly about the middle, as if losing cohesion. The skittering grew even more pronounced as the skin of the giant began to break apart, falling, chittering, to the marble stones below.

Then it all collapsed in a single moment, and the spikes and horns and fangs clattered to the floor, and the individual creatures twisted and throbbed one last time before falling completely silent and still.

Jon's legs lost all strength, and for a moment Mary held him up, then she too gave way, and they collapsed on top of the altar. Jon looked into her eyes and saw the same wonder there that he was feeling.

"Impressive." Hardy's voice cut into his relief. "I would never have thought it possible."

Jon groaned and struggled to sit upright again. Hardy and the other monks surrounded the altar. They looked human again, but their aura of menace was undiminished.

"My Masters will have to come another time," Hardy said, shrugging. "But don't kid yourself...they're coming. This is but one possible path to the earthly realms. There are many, many others."

"And they will be protected, too," Mary said.

She sounded so confident that Hardy looked deflated for a moment. Then he shrugged. "Doesn't matter. We'll make sure you won't be here to see it."

Hardy grabbed a metal bar from the wreckage scattered about the floor. The other monks had also gathered up makeshift weapons.

Jon slid off the altar to face them.

"Run, Mary," he said, keeping his voice steady. "I'll hold them off."

She dropped down beside him. "Like *that* is going to happen," she said. Somehow she had gotten hold of a long metal candlestick, which she offered to him. He took it with a grateful nod. She leaned down and came up with a thin piece of timber with a large nail on the end.

She said, "Unless your Masters can turn you back into those creatures, all I see are five mortal men. You may take us down, but not before we've taken a couple of you with us."

"You'd be doing us a favor," Hardy said. "We didn't set out to serve the Masters..." he hesitated as if he expected something to punish him for his words. When nothing happened, he grinned. "Either way, our Masters want you dead, so we can't lose."

Despite his brave words, Hardy stepped back and motioned the men behind him to attack first.

Mary struck while he was still speaking, surprising everyone, including Jon. Her swing missed. Jon hurried to follow her, and his candlestick smashed into the forehead of the first man. Very human blood spurted out, flesh tore, and bone splintered and shards dropped to the floor.

The second attacker came at them too fast to react to, swinging his thick club at Mary's waist, catching her in the side as she tried to turn and slamming her into the altar. She dropped to the floor. Jon kicked out at the man, tripping him and sending him backward into the other

187

two monks who had begun to move forward. Jon slammed the candlestick into the face of one of them, who dropped unconscious to the floor.

But it was now Jon facing three men alone, including Hardy. Mary was unmoving, bleeding from her mouth.

Hardy barked a single harsh syllable, and his two followers took a step back. Hardy swung his metal bar back and forth, as if judging its weight. Then he moved forward so fast that Jon barely had time to begin to raise the candlestick. As if in slow motion, he saw the bar coming down and realized he wouldn't be able to stop it from landing.

A blur came out of the air, and there was a loud shout. Something landed on Hardy's head, and claws dug into the man's mouth and eyes, pulling the face apart, exposing the glistening coils beneath. Hardy dropped the metal bar and screamed, his arms turning back into flailing tentacles.

A second gargoyle descended from out of the air and attacked the last two monks, ripping one of them in half, sending the other running. The gargoyle chased after him.

The smaller gargoyle still had a firm grip on Hardy and continued to pull his face apart. With a final loud plop, the head split in half, the two pieces tearing away from the neck and falling to the stone floor with a splat. The headless body toppled backward with a thump.

The little gargoyle flew over and landed on the altar, where it turned to Jon with what appeared to be a smile. "Nice to meet you at last, Jon," it said. "My name is Pretty. And my friend..." the little gargoyle looked over Jon's shoulder with an impatient frown, "...wherever he's gone off to, we call him Grotesque."

Jon didn't answer. He barely heard the creature. He was crouching over Mary, and gently shaking her shoulder. She was pale, and for a moment he couldn't tell if she was even breathing. He put his cheek to her lips and felt a wisp of breath.

Then, unexpectedly, he felt a kiss. He reared back in surprise. The light shining through the broken stained-glass windows fell across her face, the reds and greens and blues blending together in an unearthly halo. And in the middle of that glow, she opened her blue eyes and smiled at him.

Epilogue

The city officials called it a freak storm, centered over the old cathedral, with heavy flooding and high winds that shattered windows and toppled gargoyles. Five maintenance workers had been killed, but no one else was hurt.

In the aftermath, Jon accepted his scholarship to the Sagrada Familia in Barcelona. Mary decided to accompany him. Her whistleblowing had brought down one of the premier real estate businesses in the city, and shadowy connections to the underworld had been uncovered. The authorities granted her a reward that she hadn't realized existed—but they could not guarantee her safety.

Before they left for Europe, Father Michael opened the doors of the cathedral to them one last time. In the previous days, Jon had helped the new maintenance crew install the last of the gargoyles. Fortunately, the waterproof doors of the archive had held back the flood, and Jon was able to use the diagrams he found there to make sure that the gargoyles of the cathedral were configured as they were originally meant to be.

Even Pretty was back in her little niche over the room that had once been the library.

"You understand what will happen?" Jon had asked each of the guardian gargoyles. They were once again frozen in shape, but he could sense their acquiescence to his question. Only Dominic still had the ability to answer out loud, and he spoke for all of them.

"It is time."

Now, as the human survivors gathered at the newly cleaned altar, and as Father Michael took out the Book of Protective Prayers, Mary asked, "Are you sure you want to do this? What if we need the gargoyles again?"

Father Michael answered, "We only needed them in the first place because they were created by corrupted monks. If that door had not been opened, none of this would have happened."

Jon nodded in agreement. "Better that their souls move on than that they stay and become a focal point again."

And so Father Michael began to read:

"In the name of the Lord Jesus Christ, I ask, O Lord God, that you break and dissolve any and all curses, hexes, spells, seals, satanic vows and pacts, spiritual bondings and soul ties with satanic forces, evil wishes, evil desires, hereditary seals, snares, traps, lies, obstacles, deceptions, diversions, spiritual influences, and every dysfunction and disease from any source whatsoever, that have been placed upon this place.

"Father, I now place my friends and my enemies into your hands. Look with mercy upon them, and do not hold their sins against them. Anyone who has cursed me, I now bless. Anyone who has hurt me, I now forgive. For those who have persecuted me, I now pray.

"Amen and amen."

And so it was done. They looked about them, as if expecting something to be different, but the cathedral was as solid and peaceful as before.

Mary looked up one last time as she left the cathedral, at the gargoyle over the elm tree. It looked the same, but there was something missing. It was merely stone now. She felt happiness for Dominic, who had been cursed to stay frozen in purgatory forever but who had finally found release.

She took Jon's hand, and together, they walked away.

Father Michael returned to the ruined halls of the cathedral with a sense of satisfaction. Even though he still had a fight on his hands to save the cathedral, he had faith it would all work out. Amazing, having faith. If the archdiocese had wanted this cathedral torn down before, they had even more ammunition now. But he'd find a way to save it. The cathedral belonged here. *He* belonged here.

Despite the wreckage of the flood and the fight, all was right with the world. The sacred grounds were free of ghosts. Hell itself was back where it should be.

Gargoyles were now simply gargoyles, the cathedral was merely a cathedral, and he...he was a real priest.

It would all work out in the end.

She had come to Dominic asking for forgiveness.

Her name was Katherine, he remembered with a piercing clarity that stabbed at his stone heart and melted it. He remembered everything for the first time since it had happened, since the grief and guilt had clouded his mind. She was small and blonde and pretty, and she had been his friend from childhood, a friendship that had grown into a deep love.

She had gone to the man who owned their debts, and that evil man had promised to absolve their debts in full. But he'd lied, and he'd taken her and then told her she would stay with him or he would ruin her, and he would ruin Dominic, and nothing would be gained, and all would be lost.

And Katherine had believed him and gone with him, and thought that at least Dominic would escape from the consequences of her actions. But when she saw the look on his face when he walked in on them, she knew that she'd been wrong, and that the hurt to Dominic had been more than she could have ever understood.

They would face disgrace together, Dominic had told her, and they had made love again, and he had felt all the love he'd ever felt return twofold, and it had made him rise up in the deep dark of night without waking her to find their employer, their landlord, their demon, and confront him. On the balcony of the evil man's mansion they had fought, and the man had produced a pistol, which he'd fired.

Unknown to Dominic, Katherine had followed him, and that bullet found not his chest, but hers, and she had collapsed. Dominic tried to rush to her side, but his enemy had not given up his hold. With the strength of rage and love and panic, Dominic heaved the man away from him, and the villain fell backward, over the edge of the balcony and fell screaming to the rocks below.

When they had tried him for murder, Dominic, in his guilt and grief and sorrow, had not fought the charges. When hanging day had come, a priest had come to hear his confession, and instead of hanging, Dominic was led to the cathedral and turned to stone.

Now, as his soul finally became free, he remembered Katherine lying on the balcony, blood blooming from her heart like a flower, gazing up at him with love and forgiving him.

In those last moments, Dominic remembered, and he finally forgave himself. He went to the light and was wrapped in its embrace, and Katherine waited for him with open arms.

About the Author

Duncan grew up and spent most of his life in Central Oregon, the dry side of the Cascades, and whose terrain is featured in many of his books. He wrote several books out of college, including the heroic fantasy novels *Star Axe*, *Snowcastles*, and *Icetowers*. In 1984, he and his wife Linda bought Pegasus Books in downtown Bend, Oregon, which they still own and operate. They also ran a used bookstore, the Bookmark, for 15 years.

In the last five years, he's been able to get back to writing again, and found that he has a lot of pent-up creative energy. He's written numerous books for several different publishers, mostly in the horror or dark fantasy genres, though recently has been branching out into fantasy again, as well as thrillers.

BIBLIOGRAPHY

The Tuskers Series
Tuskers I: Wild Pig Apocalypse
Tuskers II: Day of the Long Pig
Tuskers III: Omnivore Wars
Tuskers IV: Rise of the Cloven

The Vampire Evolution Trilogy
Book I: Death of an Immortal
Book II: Rule of Vampire
Book III: Blood of Gold

The Virginia Reed Adventures
Led to the Slaughter
The Dead Spend No Gold
The Darkness You Fear

Other books
Star Axe
Snowcastles & Icetowers

Blood of the Succubus
Castle La Magie
Deadfall Ridge
Eden's Return
Faerie Punk
Freedy Filkins
Gargoyle Dreams
I Live Among You
Shadows over Summer House
Snaked
Takeover

Curious about other Crossroad Press books? Stop by our website:
http://crossroadpress.com
We offer quality writing
in digital, audio, and print formats.

Subscribe to our newsletter on the website homepage and receive a
free eBook.

www.ingramcontent.com/pod-product-compliance
Lightning Source LLC
Chambersburg PA
CBHW020633180626
46816CB00003B/946